KU-212-776

Barry Hines

The Price of Coal

The scripts of the two television plays
Meet the People *and* **Back to Reality**

Edited by Allan Stronach

SPENCER PARK
SCHOOL LIBRARY

Hutchinson of London

B 8691
(822 HIN)

Hutchinson & Co. (Publishers) Ltd
3 Fitzroy Square, London W1P 6JD

London Melbourne Sydney Auckland
Wellington Johannesburg and agencies
throughout the world

First published 1979

© Barry Hines 1979

The paperback edition of this book is sold subject
to the condition that it shall not, by way of trade,
or otherwise, be lent, resold, hired out, or otherwise
circulated in any form of binding or cover other than
that in which it is published and without a similar
condition being imposed on the subsequent purchaser

Set in VIP Century by Input Typesetting Ltd

Printed in Great Britain by litho at
The Anchor Press Ltd and bound by
Wm Brendon & Son Ltd, both of
Tiptree, Essex

British Library Cataloguing in Publication Data

Hines, Barry
  The price of coal.
  I. Title
  822'.9'14   PR6058.I528P
  ISBN 0 09 138560 1 cased
       0 09 138561 X paper

SAINT FRANCIS XAVIER
SIXTH FORM COLLEGE
MALWOOD ROAD SW12 8EN
LIBRARY
015015 / 822 HIN

Introduction

The two plays which are bracketed as *The Price of Coal* are intentionally complementary: *Meet the People* is a comedy about a royal visit to a colliery, and *Back to Reality* tells the tragedy of a disaster at the same pit. The same characters recur, in a similar setting, but their reactions to the two occasions reflect the dramatic contrasts of colliery life.

The inspiration for the two plays came in a context far removed from the coal face, when Barry Hines was discussing ideas for future scripts in Hyde Park on a brilliant summer afternoon in 1975. His initial proposal to his director was for a single humorous play, about the farcical preparations for a royal visit. Tony Garnett then suggested a second play, using the same characters and setting, but providing the contrast of the tragic side of colliery life. This became the plan for the two television scripts, *The Price of Coal*.

Barry Hines only began writing the plays after considerable research. For the first play, he visited several collieries on official NCB open days, and one in particular that had recently experienced a royal visit. For the second play, he read up official reports and combined their details with stories related to him by miners at various pits.

This research is backed up by a lifetime of personal experience in a mining environment. Barry Hines grew up in a colliery village, and in fact lost his grandfather in a pit disaster. His famous story of *Kes* was set against the same mining background. His writing is therefore based

entirely on observed and related detail, from the ludi-
crous incident of the brick which supports the window in
Meet the People, to the fateful football stockings in *Back to
Reality*.

The scripts were written over six months, during the
winter of 1975. Barry Hines set himself the task of working steadily through the two plays, on his usual schedule
of 9 to 5 for five days a week. They were ready for first
transmission on BBC 'Play for Today' in March 1977.

The development of *Meet the People* gives the initial
impression of a balanced representation of those for and
against the royal visit. The sense of irony is such, however, that the reader can soon detect the author's sympathy for Sid Storey, the leader of the vociferous minority
who ridiculed the visit.

In *Back to Reality* there is a link of continuity when the
play opens in a light-hearted vein again. But this mood is
abruptly broken by the news of the accident. The author's
intention is clearly to shock and surprise his audience: to
make us share the effect on the miners' families when
they are suddenly told the news from the pit.

The reviews of the television presentations were highly
complimentary, but perhaps the most valuable acclaim
came from the miners themselves. They recognized the
combination of humour and tragedy as a completely
authentic representation of pit head life.

Production notes

Both scripts have been edited to make them suitable for
either reading or production by groups in schools and col-
leges, or by drama groups of any kind.

There is a large cast in both plays, which makes them
especially suitable for group performance. Both male and
female parts are represented. Many of the same characters feature in both plays, which will help the actors to
develop a deeper identification with their roles, through
the contrasting situations of the two plays.

The scenes are short, as is usual with television plays. Some have been amalgamated for this edition, but the arrangement is still episodic, deriving from the original medium. The cuts from scene to scene will actually emphasize the consternation of the different groups of people when news breaks of the disaster.

Scenery can be minimal in both plays, as characterization is more important throughout than literal visual aids. A stylized backdrop of a pit head would be perfectly adequate, with occasional material props. The mining context could even be suggested with photographic slides or pre-recorded effects, especially for use between scenes.

In *Meet the People* all the scenes can be acted on one stage, without any danger of confusion from the changing locations.

However, in *Back to Reality* the locations change more abruptly. There are switches from place to place to give the sense of urgency, as well as returns to the same scenes over a period of time. The best solution to this production problem would be to use separate 'acting areas', which would then suggest more satisfactorily the changes in location and time. A list is provided here, allocating the scenes in *Back to Reality* to three acting areas. Acting Area 1 would be a conventional stage where most of the main scenes would be enacted; Area 2 would be set up to stage right, and Area 3 to stage left.

ACT ONE

Meet the People

Cast

(in order of appearance)

FORBES, the pit general manager
ALF MEAKIN, National Union of Mineworkers branch secretary
KEN TAYLOR, pit deputy
SID STOREY, a miner
BOB RICHARDS, pit top foreman
CARTER, the deputy manager
JIMMY, a miner
BEATSON, the under manager
TONY STOREY, Sid's eldest son, an apprentice miner
KATH, Sid's wife
MARK, Sid's youngest son
JANET, Sid's daughter
HARRY, friend of Sid's, a miner
PETE, apprentice miner
RONNIE ⎫
ALBERT ⎬ miners
ALAN ⎭
BANKSMAN, in charge of pit cage
PAINTER
FIRST APPRENTICE
SECOND APPRENTICE
RON ATKINSON, from area office
FIRST MINER
SECOND MINER

NEIL, apprentice miner
MAURICE, a miner
PADDY TRAIN DRIVER
TWO PAINTERS
SHEILA, Forbes's secretary
SIR GORDON HORROCKS
WALTER HARDY, a miner, due for retirement
MICHAEL BARTON, young apprentice
PETE, trainee miner
DICK, retired miner
BAR STEWARD
WOMAN
TWO BOMB SQUAD MEN
GEOFF ⎫
ALEC ⎬ surface workers
TOM, the telephonist
LINDA, a secretary
STAN, office worker
TEACHER
MRS FORBES

Meet the People

ACT ONE

General manager's office

*Members of the committee, i.e. representatives of manage-
ment and men, are sitting round a long table.* FORBES, *the
general manager, is the chairman and is sitting at the
head of the table. Also present are* CARTER, *the deputy manager;* BEATSON, *the under manager;* BOB RICHARDS, *the pit top
foreman;* ALF MEAKIN, *the NUM branch secretary; and,
amongst others,* SID STOREY.

FORBES: 'Item nine: Any other business. Mr Meakin said
that concessionary coal orders were building up for
delivery from Smithywood land sale, due to shortage of
suitable coal, and asked the chairman if anything could
be done about this before the winter months were on us.
Mr Forbes said he'd look into this.' Someone move this a
true and accurate record of these minutes.

ALF: I'll propose that, Mr Chairman.

KEN TAYLOR: I'll second that, Mr Chairman.

FORBES: Now, before we go on to matters arising, I've an
item of news which I think you'll find interesting. Next
month, Prince Charles is making a two-day visit to this
area. He'll be visiting Sheffield, Barnsley and one or
two other places in the area. Today I had a phone call
from the area director and he informed me that this
colliery has been chosen for an official visit. . . .

ALF: He can have a go at my job if he wants.

FORBES: In view of this, I think we ought to spend the rest of the afternoon discussing the preparations for this visit and what we're going to do about it. So would somebody like to propose a motion cancelling the present agenda. . . .

SID STOREY: I'd like to move a motion cancelling the visit.

[*Some of the men laugh*]

It's not a laughing matter, I'm serious.

BOB RICHARDS: Will he be turning up here?

CARTER: What do you mean?

RICHARDS: In here, in this office?

CARTER: We don't know yet. We haven't got the itinerary, have we?

RICHARDS: We'll have to shift these off the wall, look.

[*He indicates the nude calendar on the wall*]

CARTER: No, that's going to get repainted, that. A bit of a touch up. [*Laughs*]

FORBES: Not a bad idea.

CARTER: We haven't got the itinerary. We haven't got any idea the places he's going to be in. . . .

JIMMY: What about the muckstack?

FORBES: Well, you know my feelings about that. I want it recontoured and grassed.

BEATSON: Well, you've tried hard enough in the past.

FORBES: It doesn't matter how much we clean the yard up, it'll look nothing with that at the back of it.

CARTER: No, it wants doing.

[*Murmurs of agreement around the table*]

FORBES: If we plant the grass immediately, how long will it be before it comes through?

BEATSON: About two to three weeks, depending on the weather.

FORBES: Good. That'll give us plenty of time, then.

BEATSON: But if it rains really hard, it'll wash the seed off the banks.

FORBES: Well, we shall just have to pray that it doesn't.

JIMMY: What about the canteen at the other side of it?

SID: Oh no, they won't do anything there, because he won't be going in there, will he?

JIMMY: That's what I'm saying. Why not spend pit money for the men?

CARTER: How do you know he won't be going in there?

SID: He'll be drinking sherry in your bloody office.

CARTER: He might be going in the canteen.

FORBES: Look, we've already been designated money for a face-lift. It was going to be done, so we may as well kill two birds with one stone.

SID: You can kill three while you're at it, because I'm having nothing to do with it. If he's going to come here, he should see this pit as it is; if not, he shouldn't come at all.

TAYLOR: What about the stockyard area? It's an eyesore. There's loads of scrap that could be sold to a scrap merchant and money received from this and utilized.

CARTER: Yeh, that's a good idea.

RICHARDS: Not a bad idea.

BEATSON: And don't forget the pit baths either.

JIMMY: What about the canteen?

FORBES: We're going to do this job and we're going to be proud of it. There's nobody going to be ashamed of this pit. We're going to be proud of it, is that all right? So that's it, then. Let's cut the argument out and let's start and make this pit so we're proud of it and everybody else is. Right?

[*There is a general murmur of agreement*]

Sid's house

A terraced house in the village. Originally it was a company house, built for the miners when the mine was opened a century ago. The front door is hardly ever used. You go down the entry into the yard then across the backs of the other houses to get to the kitchen door. SID *is up on the allotment at the side of the houses. He's a keen gardener and the plot is immaculate. He's gathering a small bunch of roses, which he selects and primes carefully. He is puffing contentedly on his pipe.*

SID *walks down towards the house, carrying his bunch of roses. As he reaches his back door,* TONY *rushes out, carrying his snap tin.* SID *looks at his watch.*

SID: Off early, aren't you?

TONY: I'm just popping in to see Linda.

SID: You'll be popping in there once too often.

[TONY *laughs and goes on his way.* SID *goes in to his wife,* KATH. *Their son,* MARK, *aged nine, is in the living room watching cricket on the television*]

KATH: Come on, Sid, you're going to be late.

SID: Here you are. Beautiful, them, aren't they?

KATH: Yes. Put them on the sink and I'll see to them after.

[SID *selects his favourite out of the bunch and puts it into a small vase. He goes over to his son*]

SID: All right, son?

MARK: Right, dad.

SID: Who's batting?

MARK: Yorkshire.

SID: How many are they?

MARK: Fifty-nine for one. Good match, though, from what I've seen.

SID: Not a bloody good picture, though, is it?

MARK: No. Why can't we get a colour telly?

SID: Ah, it's going back to Wiggy's shop soon, I'll tell you that. . . . Is Boycott out yet?

MARK: No, he's playing well – so are Yorkshire.

SID: Good.

MARK: Look at that. Look at 'em. On our telly they look like pygmies.

[KATH *brings in* SID'S *lunch*]

KATH: Here you are, love.

SID: Cheers. Put it on there.

MARK: Where's mine, mum?

KATH: I'll get you yours, Mark, when your dad's gone to work.

[JANET, *their daughter, comes into the room.* KATH *looks at her in surprise*]

KATH: Oh, hello, love. What're you doing home?

JANET: I forgot my cookery money.

KATH: How much do you want?

JANET: Oh, fifty pence.

KATH: Fifty pence, Sid, for cookery. Oh, and Janet, you can use that other fifty pence to bring me a loaf. . . .

[JANET *goes.* KATH *tidies the room*]

MARK: Dad, you know that big 'do' they're having at your pit?

SID: Yes.

MARK: Shaun Chappell says anybody can go down, and he's going down with his grandma.

SID: Not unless his grandma's the Queen, he's not.

KATH: I've heard that as well, Sid. They say that when all the VIPs have gone, they're going to let the general public down for a look.

SID: No, love, that's only on Open Days. This is an official visit.

KATH: They say they're making a good job of the pit yard, though, Sid.

SID: They ought to be, there's enough of them at it. I've never seen anything like it. Folks would think royalty were coming or something.

[HARRY *knocks on the door and comes straight in*]

KATH: Morning, Harry.

HARRY: All right, love.

KATH: Harry's here, Sid.

SID: I'll just watch this last ball. . . .

[HARRY *also watches the television as* KATH *continues speaking*]

KATH: You've got over it now, Harry – the visit?

HARRY: Got over it! You know, every time I think about it, it's like having one of you're back teeth pulled.

KATH: Aye, you may be right.

SID: That bloke there reckons he's a fast bowler and I've seen faster bowlers on the green down at our club.

KATH: Oh, get off to work.

[*The two men leave the house and set out for work*]

MARK: (*Loudly*) Boycott's out!

SID: He wants to be!

[*The two men hurry back inside to watch the action*

replay. KATH *continues to clean the room. The two men are furious at having missed Boycott being caught out*]

SID: The silly chuff. What's he want to be hooking for at this time of day?

HARRY: Hooking? He wants. . . .

KATH: Hey! You can stop that language and save it till you get to the pit.

HARRY: That's all I needed. Sunny afternoon like this. Afternoon shift and now Boycott's out. I might as well jump in the bloody reservoir. . . .

The pit gate

SID *and* HARRY *arrive at the pit entrance. They notice a new painted sign and stop.* SID *reads it aloud.*

SID: 'NCB South Yorkshire Area. MILTON UNIT. *E Tenebris Lux*.'

HARRY: How long's that been up?

SID: Put it up Friday.

HARRY: 'Milton Unit, NCB South Yorkshire Area. *E Tenebris Lux*'? Bloody hell.

SID: Latin, that.

HARRY: Latin?

SID: Ah, it means out of the shadows comes the light.

HARRY: Bloody hell. Where'd you get that from?

SID: Our Tony.

HARRY: Your Tony.

SID: He did a bit of Latin at school.

HARRY: What's he doing down the pit, then, if he knows Latin?

SID: Didn't do it for long, did he? He didn't have much

choice really. He packed it in. You needs seven GCEs to get a job sweeping up, these days.

[PETE, *an apprentice miner, enters carrying a fresh sapling to put into a hole he has already dug. He is wearing his pit helmet*]

SID: Hey up, Pete, it's a tree you're planting there, you know, not a daffodil.

PETE: What do you mean?

SID: Look at the size of that hole. It wants to be twice as deep as that and a lot wider. Look, you've got to give room for those roots to spread or else it'll die.

PETE: It's only for the royal visit. I mean, after that it's done with, in't it?

HARRY: Now, come on. If you're going to do the job, do it right.

PETE: I'm bleeding pissed off with gardening. I came here to be a miner, didn't I?

SID: You should think yourself lucky you've got such an enlightened employer, training you in all these different skills.

PETE: Is that right? Anyway, get off the garden. I've been here all morning digging this garden and then there's you two come and. . . .

SID: Does you good. You can come and do mine when you've finished that.

PETE: Likely!

SID: Another thing. Do you know that by planting that tree you're ensuring the economic future of this country?

PETE: How do you work that out?

SID: Well, you know where coal comes from, don't you – how it's made?

PETE: Course I do. We did geography, you know.

SID: Well, how's it made then?

PETE: It's made with trees, dying off, and after millions of years it forms coal, don't it?

SID: Well, there you go then. Stocks don't last for ever, do they? By planting that tree, you're safeguarding the economic future of the coal industry for the next two million years.

PETE: Don't be so daft.

SID: I'm telling you, it's what's known as long-term planning.

HARRY: Come on, silly bugger, or you'll have him as daft as you.

SID: Have they recruited our Tony into the Forestry Commission as well yet?

PETE: Aye, he's in the wood business. He's stocking chocks up there.

SID: What are you doing planting that tree with your hat on, anyway.

PETE: It's regulations, isn't it? You can't take them off, can you?

HARRY: Anyway, if you want that thing to grow you'd better get a bigger hole.

SID: He's right, you know.

PETE: I'd better go and look for a bigger spade then.

[SID *and* HARRY *laugh. They go off one way as* PETE *goes the other*]

General manager's office

FORBES *is on the telephone. Two painters enter and cover the office with dustsheets in preparation for painting.*

FORBES: . . . It is that. I'm pleased they don't call me that.

I get called enough names by the men as it is.... Thursday ... next Thursday. What time?....

[*He writes down the information*]

... and he's from the Palace itself, is he? ... Well, so far so good, touch wood....

[*There is a knock on the door.* CARTER *and* BEATSON *enter*]

Come in! ... righto, Joe. I'll fix that up. Thanks. Cheerio.

[*He puts the phone down*]

CARTER: Hey, they're making a good job of these offices, aren't they?

FORBES: Beautiful.

CARTER: I think I'll bring a bed in and sleep in mine. It's better than our house.

FORBES: Now then. I just wondered how things were progressing. We want to keep on top of everything, don't we?

CARTER: Yes.

FORBES: Now, are there any difficulties – any fresh problems anywhere?

BEATSON: No, except there's a lot of paint getting pinched. They're just unloading it off the lorries and it's just standing around unattended. The fellas are just walking past and lifting it.

FORBES: Well, that's got to stop. The minute that paint comes off the lorries, I want it put under lock and key, because I'm not having every bloody pigeon loft and garden shed painted at the NCB's expense.... Now, underground. Has the stone come for that plaque yet?

CARTER: They've promised it for this afternoon.

FORBES: Well, follow that up. We don't want to leave jobs like that to the last minute.

SPENCER PARK
SCHOOL LIBRARY

BEATSON: Have you got your curtains?

CARTER: Aye, curtains are all done. They've made a good job of them an' all. They just want putting up now.

FORBES: Listen. This afternoon I've got Ron Atkinson coming over from area office. Now what I propose to do is the four of us will have a walk round the yard and see if we can spot any little detail we might have missed or we can improve on. Ron's an outsider, so he might see something we've missed – us being on the premises all day, see. Now, the emissary's coming up from the Palace next Thursday to plot and plan everything. We're not sure what route he'll take yet, but we've a rough idea. Right, you can get off now. I'll give you a buzz when Ron comes.

BEATSON: Right, see you later.

CARTER: Hey, what's your office like? I can't find a bloody thing in mine....

[*They go out.* FORBES *picks up the phone and rings the switchboard*]

FORBES: Is Bob there? ... Well, I want him. That you, Bob? Forbes. Listen, what's Tom doing? ... Well, that can wait, that can. I want you to get him, tell him to give my car a good wash down and have it outside of my office for three o'clock. OK?

The pit head

SID, HARRY, RONNIE, ALBERT *and* ALAN *are waiting at the pit head ready to descend in the cage. They are dressed in their pit clothes and carrying their lamps. The pit head gear is being painted by a team of* PAINTERS.

RONNIE: What are we doing here, then? They don't look like Coal Board painters, do they?

ALBERT: Somebody told me it's the same firm that paints Blackpool Tower every year.

RONNIE: It looks a bit better anyway. I bet it's not been painted since it was put up.

HARRY: It's forced to have been. This pit's more than a hundred years old.

ALBERT: I'm telling you, I've been here thirty-eight years come November and it's not been done in my time.

RONNIE: They're doing a good job anyway.

SID: I could do with some of that to paint my chicken run.

ALAN: I wish I were doing that this afternoon instead of going where I'm going.

[*They all agree*]

ALBERT: And me.

[BANKSMAN *enters to search them for cigarettes and matches*]

BANKSMAN: How do, Ronnie?

RONNIE: Fine thanks.

BANKSMAN: How's Yorkshire going on?

SID: They were eighty-five for two when we came out.

BANKSMAN: Is Boycott out?

SID: Ah, just as we left.

HARRY: Don't talk about it.

BANKSMAN: How many did he get?

SID: Forty-four.

BANKSMAN: Can't grumble at that.

HARRY: Who can't?

[BANKSMAN *continues frisking*]

RONNIE: How will you go on when you're frisking Him, then?

BANKSMAN: Don't you worry about Him. Same as you, you know, just the same. Feel in his pockets. Just the same as this.

ALAN: He could have half a ton of dynamite up his back and you'd say nothing.

BANKSMAN: Get away. He wouldn't go down with dynamite on. He don't take contraband like you idiots.

SID: He's more likely to than us, isn't he? He don't know anything about the job. We work here. We know what could happen.

BANKSMAN: They tell me he doesn't smoke, does he?

ALBERT: Tell me he smokes Woodbines.

RONNIE: No, I heard he rolled his own.

HARRY: I wonder if he saves coupons.

SID: He's bound to. Inflation's hitting them, you know, same as us. You've only got to read the papers to know that.

HARRY: I bet he's saving up for one of these new lawnmowers. They say they've got a lot of grass at the back of their house.

SID: Forty million quid he's worth.

ALAN: Never.

SID: He is. He gets most of it from the Duchy of Cornwall.

ALBERT: Who's she?

SID: It's land, you daft sod. If they ever tax brains you'll get a rebate, you Albert. He's got a lot of land in Devon and Cornwall. And big estates in London. The best is, though, you know when he got that rise in 1973, Parliament agreed to pay his widow sixty thousand pounds a year. That's over a thousand pounds a week of taxpayers' money.

RONNIE: How do you mean, his widow? He's not bloody married.

SID: Yes, but she'll still want looking after when he goes.

ALBERT: A thousand pounds a week. How much does an ordinary widow get?

SID: Nineteen pound fifty.

HARRY: Come on Leslie Welch, the cage is here.

ALAN: Who's Leslie Welch?

HARRY: Don't you know? No, of course, you're not old enough to know Leslie Welch.

ALBERT: He knows more about Racquel Welch, that one.

ALAN: I've heard of him.

[*The cage is heard coming up. The men hand the* BANKSMAN *their metal checks and start to queue to get into the cage as the last shift get out*]

ALBERT: Has the Snowcem come yet, Arthur?

BANKSMAN: Snowcem? What're you talking about?

ALBERT: They tell me they're sending ten thousand gallons of Snowcem to whitewash the shaft for the 'do'.

BANKSMAN: Don't talk wet.

RONNIE: Hey, they're going to paint the cage, though, aren't they?

BANKSMAN: Ah, they're going to paint it last, though, so you buggers don't muck it up.

[*They begin to get into the cage*]

RONNIE: Thanks very much. I hope you've gone home when we come out.

BANKSMAN: I'll have gone home and be watching television.

HARRY: I hope it pisses down.

[*The* BANKSMAN *presses the bell for the cage to descend the shaft*]

The pit yard 1

PAINTER *enters carefully painting a white line. Two young* APPRENTICES *carrying a heavy piece of 'ring' enter. The one walking backwards steps on to the line.*

PAINTER: Keep off that line. Watch where you're going. You big daft pillock! Look what you've done! Keep your foot up. Don't put that foot down!

FIRST APPRENTICE: Well, how could I see, carrying that?

PAINTER: You've heard what Forbes said. We want this yard cleaning up so's Prince Charles can eat his dinner off it. Keep that leg up.

[*The* APPRENTICE *is dutifully hopping up and down on one foot*]

FIRST APPRENTICE: Don't blame me!

SECOND APPRENTICE: He's got to put his foot down.

PAINTER: Are you two blind, or are you bloody daft, or what?

SECOND APPRENTICE: Who do you think you are?

PAINTER: Never mind, I'm painting this bloody line. Don't put your foot down!

[*They struggle off, half-hopping, not knowing exactly what to do*]

PAINTER: Lads like them are all the same. Just look at this, what they've done.

[FORBES, CARTER, BEATSON *enter along with* RON ATKINSON *from area office*]

ATKINSON: The whole approach to the pit is one hundred per cent improvement. You've made a good job of it.

[*They have stopped and are admiring the newly planted trees and the freshly painted headgear and buildings*]

FORBES: Just look at those saplings. In another few years, when they're established, it'll be just like driving up to a stately home. I think he'll be proud when he comes.

ATKINSON: I would have thought so. You've put a lot of work into it.

CARTER: Yes.

FORBES: What d'you think of it, then?

ATKINSON: Well, it looks absolutely spot on as far as I can see, Stan.

FORBES: Well, don't you notice anything different?

ATKINSON: I can't see anything ... just a minute – the old stack. You've had it recontoured.

FORBES: I should think so. Just look at it. Just look at that lot. Don't it look better?

ATKINSON: Have you had it grassed as well?

FORBES: Yes. It's going to look a picture, this is.

ATKINSON: It's a great improvement, Stan.

FORBES: Oh, when the grass is up on it, it'll look just like a great big green hill. I bet you can see grass coming through now.

[FORBES *gets down on his hands and knees and looks up the angle of the tip.* ATKINSON *does the same and after a pause the two deputy managers get down with them, so that all four men are in a line on all fours looking up the tip*]

FORBES: Yeh, you can. Look there. Look at that lot. Look there. Get down. Look, just like a green haze there, look.

[*Two miners enter.* FIRST MINER *just shakes his head*]

SECOND MINER: What are they doing?

FIRST MINER: I don't know. Like a team of bloody ostriches getting ready for a race.

SECOND MINER:　Silly sods! [*They walk away laughing*]

[*The men stand up and brush their knees*]

FORBES:　Right. Now let's look at the offices.

[*The four men of the management go off*]

The pit yard 2

Two apprentices, NEIL *and* TONY – SID'S *elder son – are painting a wall. They are bored with the job.* TONY *starts flicking paint at the wall with his brush, then his actions become more vigorous and he starts slashing it on and dabbing at it, making random streaks on the wall.* NEIL *steps away from him.*

NEIL:　Hey, don't do that, you dirty sod. These were clean on this morning, now I've got paint all over me.

TONY:　Action painting – that's action painting.

NEIL:　What's action painting?

TONY:　Haven't you seen it on the telly?

NEIL:　No.

TONY:　Well, they get their brushes like this and they splash it on like that and then they get motor-bikes and ride them across. Then they roll nude women across.

NEIL:　Nude women? ... I'd like to roll Sharon Marshall across it. Be nice, wouldn't it? Here, did you see her dancing last night?

TONY:　Ah, it weren't bad, was it?

NEIL:　They were like two kids playing under a blanket.

[BOB RICHARDS *appears*]

RICHARDS:　What are you messing about at now?

NEIL:　Painting the wall, like you told us to do.

RICHARDS:　And what's that supposed to be?

TONY: Modern art that, Bob, to brighten the place up a bit for when Prince Charles comes.

RICHARDS: I'll brighten you up in a minute. Playing about like that. Now get that covered up and get some paint on there and try and do it properly. This is the bloody National Coal Board not the National Art Gallery.

[*He walks away*]

NEIL: A right philistine. He talks a load of balls.

RICHARDS: What did you say?

NEIL: I said we're going to need a lot of turpentine to get this paint off our overalls.

RICHARDS: Oh. [*But suspiciously*]

[*They all exit*]

The pit yard 3

Outside the office block.

FORBES: You can see what they're going to look like, can't you, when they're all painted up? It'll be all right, won't it?

[*Suddenly, the two* APPRENTICES *run past – one carrying the other who has put his foot in the paint. The four men look astonished*]

ATKINSON: What the hell's happening?

FORBES: Oi! Here, come here.

FIRST APPRENTICE: Me?

FORBES: Both of you.

FIRST APPRENTICE: What have we done?

FORBES: Get yourselves here and shut up. What're you pratting about for?

APPRENTICES: We're going to the baths, Mr Forbes.

FORBES: I know you're going to the baths, Mr Forbes. Who do you think you are? Lester Piggott?

SECOND APPRENTICE: He's just giving me a lift up. We've just been down in the stockyard.

FORBES: I can see he's giving you a lift up. But why are you going like this?

SECOND APPRENTICE: Because I trod in something.

FORBES: I've trod in summat many a time, but nobody gives me a ride. What've you trod in?

SECOND APPRENTICE: Some paint – down in stockyard. On a white line. . . .

FORBES: Ah, because you've been pratting about again, you two, haven't you?

FIRST APPRENTICE: No, we have not ... we've been doing our job.

FORBES: I'm not talking to you. You shut up a minute. What's he sent you up to do? Get that paint off?

SECOND APPRENTICE: Yes.

FORBES: Right. In there, get it off and get back up there and stop messing about. Get your work done. Get in there.

[*The* APPRENTICES *move off towards the baths, muttering*]

FORBES: ... Well, we'll try and get back to reality, eh?

ATKINSON: Yes.

FORBES: He'll get out over there. Now, we'll be lined up about here, I should imagine. Eh?

BEATSON: Yes, yes.

ATKINSON: What about the red carpet? Are you going to have one down?

[FORBES *looks at his two deputies. They don't know either*]

FORBES: I don't know. What do you think? I don't know.

ATKINSON: It's up to you – I suppose it's the usual practice.

FORBES: Well, the emissary'll be up soon. We can ask him what the procedure is.

BEATSON: I think we ought to order a length, though, just in case.

FORBES: You think so?

BEATSON: I think we ought to.

FORBES: Get your book out, then. I'll just pace it out to give us a rough idea. Right?

[FORBES *strides out the distance*]

FORBES: One, two, three, four, five, six – seven. Seven yards. Tell you what, make it ten – ten yards.

BEATSON: Ten yards of what?

FORBES: I don't know. [*Pause*] Stair carpet. Maroon stair carpet, I suppose. Tell you what: best plan, get Sheila – tell her to see to it. She'll know what to do on a job like this. All right?

CARTER: I know! Why don't we put down a roll of belting, eh? It won't cost us a penny then.

FORBES: Don't you think I've just had enough with them two without you starting?

CARTER: Well, I don't think we should go to any extra expenditure. We don't want to antagonize the men.

FORBES: Why should it do that? There's ninety-nine per cent of the men wanting this visit.

CARTER: They'll not all welcome it, will they?

FORBES: You've just got a few, haven't you – knockers – but all the rest want it. They're proud he's coming to this pit. We're not going to spoil it, are we, for the sake of a bit of bloody carpeting?

BEATSON: Right.

Underground

SID, HARRY, RONNIE, ALBERT *and* ALAN *have arrived underground and approach* MAURICE, *who is painting two decorative rings at each side of the flanges of an air pipe which runs along one wall. He is concentrating and taking great care with the rings. The pipe is white; the rings are red. The men watch him working.*

SID: Hello, Maurice. All right, son?

MAURICE: Oh, hello, Sid.

ALBERT: Hey, what you doing here? Painting again?

SID: They're bringing two tubs of flowered wallpaper down on the next draw. Gaffer says you've to put them up as soon as you've finished that.

MAURICE: I tell you what, I'd rather put wallpaper up than do this job any day.

[*The* PADDY TRAIN DRIVER *enters*]

ALBERT: Has it come yet, then?

MAURICE: Has what come?

ALBERT: That outfit you're getting.

MAURICE: Which outfit's that?

ALBERT: Velvet overalls, white helmet, matching kid gloves and dicky bow. For him when he gets here.

DRIVER: Come on, let's have you on the paddy.

RONNIE: How are we going to go on when the paddy's not here? How we going to get to work?

DRIVER: How'd you mean?

RONNIE: They're taking paddy train out, you know.

DRIVER: How can they?

RONNIE: They've got a tub painted white, man, and they're looking for four white pit ponies.

ALBERT: They've got some foam rubber cushions covered

in red material for him to sit on when he's in the train.

RONNIE: I should hope so as well, because we can't have him sitting on anything cold and hard and finishing up with piles.

[*They all laugh as they go to get the paddy train*]

General manager's office

FORBES *leads the way into the office.* CARTER *takes their pit helmets from them. The* PAINTERS *are just finishing the office.*

FORBES: Sheila! Tea for four in five minutes please. Well, what d'you think then, Stan? [*He sits down*]

ATKINSON: Very nice. Very nice. It'll be like a five-star hotel when it's finished.

FORBES: Now, lads, how's it going?

PAINTERS: All right.

FORBES: We thought we'd keep it this colour. I had a word with Mrs Forbes. She said no fancy colours, like, you know.

ATKINSON: It's nice and clean.

CARTER: How are you going?

PAINTER: Great ... smashing.

FORBES: We're keeping these lads at it.

CARTER: They'll be pleased – good for their overtime. Eh?

PAINTER: Yeh, great.

FORBES: [*Getting back to business*] When we've been changed and we get to the pit head, I'm going to make him a presentation.

ATKINSON: What sort of a presentation?

FORBES: I've had him a deputy's yardstick made. I've had

it polished up by one of the engineers and capped with silver.

[FORBES *takes the deputy's stick out of his desk and unwraps it to show* ATKINSON]

ATKINSON: Very nice. Is that real silver?

FORBES: Course it is. Look, there's the maker's initials. . . .

[SHEILA *brings the tea in*]

ATKINSON: Worth a bob or two that, you know.

FORBES: Yes, I know, but it'll make a nice little memento and I think he'll appreciate it, don't you?

ATKINSON: I do indeed.

[SHEILA *pours the tea and then goes out*]

FORBES: And I've also had this made up for him.

[*He unwraps a photograph album*]

This is an album of photographs, old photographs, of royalty visiting the pits in the area years ago. I thought we'd make an album up and. . . .

ATKINSON: Nice collection, isn't it?

FORBES: It'll make a nice reading for him – he'll be able to have an hour or two when he's at sea, looking at this, thinking about us.

[*They laugh*]

BEATSON: That's the Queen. . . . Which Queen'll that be?

FORBES: That's Queen Mary, that.

BEATSON: Hope he'll like that.

CARTER: Very nice. Very nice.

ATKINSON: Was it during the 1912 visit that there was a big disaster at a nearby pit? Cadeby Main, wasn't it?

FORBES: Yes, on the same day. While they were at Silverwood there was an explosion at Cadeby and there were

eighty-six men and lads killed. I've got it here somewhere. I was going to include it in the album, but I had
second thoughts, because when you read it you'll
understand why.

ATKINSON: [*Reads*] 'A happy event was marred by terrible
rumours of a pit tragedy at Cadeby Main, where
eighty-six men and boys were killed. In the evening the
King and Queen arrived unexpectedly at Cadeby Main
colliery to express their sympathy to the bereaved
wives and families. Then they returned to Wentworth
where they were staying with the Fitzwilliam family.'
Bad luck, that.

FORBES: What?

ATKINSON: That disaster happening on the same day as
their visit.

FORBES: Oh, yes, yes. Terrible, that.

[SHEILA *enters*]

SHEILA: Mr Forbes, Mr Horrocks is here. Mr Horrocks
from the Palace.

FORBES: Right. OK. Right, Sheila, show him in straightaway.

[HORROCKS *enters*]

HORROCKS: Good morning, gentlemen.

FORBES: Good morning, Sir Gordon, I'm, er, Forbes, general manager of the pit.

[*They shake hands*]

FORBES: Geoff ... Geoff Carter, my deputy manager. Sir
Gordon Horrocks, the equerry from the Palace. And
Philip Beatson, my under manager.

BEATSON: Hello.

[*The* EQUERRY *is introduced to everyone else in the
room*]

HORROCKS: Well, gentlemen, we have a very tight schedule on this visit, a lot of engagements to fulfil. So it is essential that every section of this programme should be timed to the minute. Now, the helicopter will land at ten-thirty precisely. . . .

[FORBES, CARTER *and* BEATSON *look at each other*]

FORBES: Helicopter?

HORROCKS: Yes, is there anything wrong?

FORBES: No, you've just taken us by surprise, that's all. We naturally thought he'd be travelling by car.

HORROCKS: No, we nearly always use a helicopter for these meet-the-people tours. You see you get the maximum number of visits in a given area and it minimizes the travelling time.

FORBES: Well, yes, I can appreciate that.

HORROCKS: Now, where do you suggest we have the landing patch?

FORBES: Well, the pit yard itself would seem the ideal spot.

HORROCKS: Yes, that's possible.

FORBES: There's no tall buildings and you're well clear of the headgears and there are no wires. . . .

BEATSON: What about the markings? Will it have to be marked out at all?

HORROCKS: Yes, you need to have a large white 'H' painted on the ground, which is perfectly easy for the pilot to pick up when he comes in to land.

FORBES: The pilot? I thought he took the controls himself.

HORROCKS: Well, he does sometimes on more leisurely occasions. Now, immediately after touch-down, you will have the introduction of the Coal Board personnel and officials of the mining unions and associations.

FORBES: Yes, yes.

HORROCKS: And that, I presume, will take place just out-side here, because the next port of call will be the offices.

FORBES: Yes, yes, that's the idea of it, yes.

HORROCKS: Now, I wonder if somebody could make a note of all this, could they?

FORBES: Phil, do you mind?

BEATSON: All right, yes.

FORBES: Thank you, very much.

[BEATSON *takes a notebook and pencil out of his pocket and writes down the various times and instructions that the* EQUERRY *gives. The* EQUERRY *takes out his stop-watch and starts it*]

HORROCKS: Right, ten-thirty touch-down.

BEATSON: Ten-thirty touch-down.

HORROCKS: That's right.

CARTER: Have you got that, Phil?

BEATSON: Yes. . . .

[*They begin to go through the motions of the visit*]

HORROCKS: Now, Mr Forbes, you will walk forward and be presented, then you'll proceed with His Royal Highness to the official party.

[*He starts walking*]

At ten-thirty-two, introduction of the official party. And how many men have you got actually in the line-up, Mr Forbes?

FORBES: Well, I really couldn't tell you, Sir Gordon, off hand, but I've got them all outside. Shall I bring them in and line them up?

HORROCKS: If you would, please. It would make it much more accurate.

[FORBES *hurries out of the office.* SHEILA *moves over to*

speak to the EQUERRY]

SHEILA: Excuse me, Sir Gordon, do you find everything is going to plan for you?

HORROCKS: Yes, it's going very well, I think, yes.

SHEILA: I wonder if you'd pardon me for saying this, sir, but you do very much remind me of the Duke of Edinburgh. Do you mind me saying so?

HORROCKS: Really? Well, I don't think he'd be very pleased, because he's very much younger than I am.

SHEILA: Oh, you very much resemble him, very much indeed. I've just been saying I think you very much resemble him, very much so.

HORROCKS: Well, don't say a word, but I think I'm a little taller than he is, that's the only thing.

SHEILA: Is that a fact? Well. . . .

[CARTER *and* BEATSON *are standing to one side*]

CARTER: I'll tell you one thing, Phil.

BEATSON: What's that, Geoff?

CARTER: It's a bloody good thing this pit's not near a canal.

BEATSON: Why not?

CARTER: Well, he would have come in his cruiser, wouldn't he? Think of the bloody job we'd have had on widening that.

[*The people to be presented enter the office and start sorting themselves out for the line-up.* FORBES *takes the* EQUERRY *along the line of men practising the presentation. The* EQUERRY *is substituting for* PRINCE CHARLES]

FORBES: . . . and this gentleman here, this is Walter Hardy. He's one of our longest serving employees. He started work in the mines at thirteen. He's due for retirement next month after forty-one years of loyal service.

WALTER: Loyal service! I'd no other bloody choice.

FORBES: Walter, you've been already told twice, you don't speak unless His Royal Highness speaks to you first.

WALTER: Sorry about that, sir.

HORROCKS: All you have to do is to bow slightly and shake hands and wait for Prince Charles to hold out his hand before you take it. You understand?

WALTER: Yes, sir.

HORROCKS: And should His Royal Highness speak to you, you will address him as 'sir'.

FORBES: And I hope when the day comes, Walter, you're going to have your teeth in.

WALTER: Well, I want a new set. These are loose. I sound like a bloody trotting pony when I've got the buggers in.

FORBES: Walter! I know the Prince is a nautical man and I know he knows all the words, but he's going to hear none from you, or anyone else on that day, so remember that, will you?

WALTER: Yes, sir.

FORBES: Right. . . . And this is Michael Barton, one of our youngest apprentices. He's a real good lad; he's coming on real well. But there's one thing I'd like to tell him. Do us a favour, Michael – get your hair cut for the day, please, will you?

MICHAEL: I had it cut yesterday.

FORBES: When?

MICHAEL: Yesterday.

FORBES: Turn round, lad. Well, the only thing I can say – he's robbed you.

HORROCKS: Well. I think that will be all right so far. Everything seems to be in order nearly. Let's go and try it out in the yard itself, shall we?

FORBES: Yes. Probably be for the best if we did. This way. . . .

[*They all go out*]

The pit yard 4

PETE, *the trainee miner, is painting a large 'H' in the middle of the pit yard. This area has been roped off to keep people off the wet paint.* NEIL *and* TONY *approach him and stand watching.*

TONY: Hey up, what're you doing?

NEIL: Making a five-a-side pitch or something?

PETE: Wish I was.

NEIL: What is it then?

PETE: It's for a helicopter. He's coming by helicopter. Didn't you know?

TONY: Helicopter? No, I didn't know that.

PETE: Manager didn't either. There's been a right flap on. He's had me hosing it all down, brushing it. I've been doing it all day and him running in and out of his office to see if I were doing it right.

NEIL: By the look of it, I thought it was a bloody five-a-side pitch or summat.

[BOB RICHARDS, *the pit top foreman, approaches*]

RICHARDS: Hey! Where you two supposed to be working?

NEIL: Oh, we've just come down from the fitters shop. We're off up to stockyard now.

RICHARDS: Well, before you go, I've got a little job for you. But I'd better go and make it right with Harry first.

TONY: What do you want us to do, then?

RICHARDS: Well, I'll tell you what I want you to do. There's two tubs behind the offices. I want you to bring them round the front and stand one either side of the door, then go to the stores and get a wheelbarrow. I want you to fill them up with soil.

NEIL: What, pit tubs full of soil?

RICHARDS: Flower tubs, you dozy bugger.

NEIL: Oh, are there some flowers there, then?

RICHARDS: It would look great with two pit tubs in front of the office, wouldn't it? Mr Forbes wants them brought around because he wants some flowers and decoration at the front of the office. Get away and get it done now. Don't hurry, will you?

[*They go off*]

RICHARDS: You get on with your lines and try and keep them straight.

[PETE *gets on with his painting*]

ACT TWO

The Working Men's Club

People are sitting round two tables in the Working Men's Club. At one is SID, ALBERT *and* RONNIE. *At the other is* ALF MEAKIN, *the union branch secretary, and* DICK, *a retired miner.* SID, ALBERT *and* RONNIE *are in the middle of a story-telling session.*

SID: He got that drunk in the beer tent they had to take him home in the pit ambulance. Can you imagine our Edna's face when he rolled up outside in that? She thought something serious had happened to him. So they opened the back doors and he rolls out singing and shouting. She kicked him from backside to breakfast time right across the road and upstairs to bed. . . . Got a right temper, her, you know, when she gets going. She wouldn't let him out of the house for a week.

ALBERT: Aye, but you don't know the reason, do you? He'd kept her waiting over an hour. He'd promised to take her down the pit – they could go down that day.

RONNIE: She didn't miss anything then, did she?

[*A game of snooker finishes. The players put their cues back into the rack.* ALBERT *gets up and takes a cue.* SID *joins him*]

RONNIE: A waste of time for me, those open days. It's all dressing the pit up for folks that live in the village just to come and have a look.

SID: It's better having an open day and folks from the district coming than what we're having. Somebody that's got nothing to do with the pit. I mean, that's a bloody waste of time and money, that is.

RONNIE: I wouldn't say that because if you've got somebody important coming to the pit, like we've got, I mean it's bloody royalty, in'it – you've got to dress it up a bit.

SID: I'm not talking about putting a bit of a show on. I'm talking about spending thousands of pounds of public's money on a visit that's going to last no more than two hours. I thought there was supposed to be a crisis on. Telling us we're supposed to be tightening our belts. How does he expect people to take any notice of that when they see all this lot going on?

ALBERT: Mind you, I think people like it. A bit of pomp and ceremony – I think it brightens life up a bit, doesn't it?

SID: It's like the other day on the tele, he were on, Chancellor of Exchequer at one of these banquets. He stood there with his bloody white jacket on and dicky bow. I'm not kidding you, he's telling us what a state we're in and he'd just finished eating a meal that'd cost more than some blokes earn in a week. I mean, there were that much grub on that table they had to have four hydraulic chocks to hold the bugger up. They must think we're stupid, them.

[ALF MEAKIN, *the branch secretary, is sitting at the next table. He has been listening to the previous conversation*]

ALF: Oh give up, Sid. You know as well as I do that the money isn't just spent for the visit.

SID: What, just a coincidence is it, then, that they decided to do our pit up just when he was coming?

ALF: I don't know how they decided, but I do know that the money's there. All they've done is accelerated the spending of it, that's all. . . .

SID: Don't talk bloody stupid.

ALF: I reckon it's a good thing.

RONNIE: I agree with you, Alf. You figure it out for yourself. That pit's been in a hell of a bloody state for years. You know it and I know it.

SID: That's not the point, Ronnie. If all this fuss is worth making, it's worth making for us, isn't it? It's us that live here. We have to see the bloody place every day, don't we?

[DICK, *a retired miner, has been sitting at the same table as* ALF, *listening*]

DICK: What's bloody royalty ever done for us? They're only bloody parasites.

RONNIE: You shut your face.

DICK: You shut your bloody face or I'll take you outside and show you what's what. I've worked there forty-three years and they never painted the bugger for me, did they?

ALBERT: Oh, come on. Are we having a drink or are we getting our gloves on?

ALF: It's an honour for this pit to be chosen and most of

the men think so as well.

SID: Honour my backside. I'll tell you why they chose our pit, shall I?

ALF: Get lost.

SID: Shall I tell you why they chose our pit?

ALF: Go on, then, clever bugger.

SID: Because they knew that our union branch officials are soft and that they won't oppose it.

ALF: Why should we oppose it? The men agreed to it, didn't they?

SID: The men had nothing to do with it. You never said a dicky bird. You just passed it.

ALF: They could've said something if they wanted to. Everybody knew about it.

SID: Look, any branch official worth his salt would've rejected that proposal and then come and told us about it and see what we thought about it. Can you imagine them lined up at Langley or Woodseats collieries?

ALF: They're bloody communists, that's why.

SID: Who are?

ALF: Tommy Lunn and Sam Haywood. Everybody knows that.

SID: You wouldn't call 'em that to their faces, would you?

ALF: All right then, they might not be Party members but you know what I mean.

SID: Aye, I know just what you mean. You mean troublemakers, don't you? And that's a term you use to discredit anybody who's not walking hand in glove with the management. They're not even members of the Labour Party, never mind communists, half of that lot. They're just branch officials who put the interests of men first and that's what they're elected for, in'it? That's their job and anybody who don't do that should be out on his backside.

ALBERT: Come on, we're not going to waste our time talking to such as him about. . . .

SID: Nay, Albert, we've got to stop sucking up to these buggers because we insult ourselves when we do, we do ourselves down.

ALF: You're an extremist, you, Sid.

SID: Look, they don't fool me, riding round in their bleeding Rolls-Royces, waving and shaking hands with folks. There's never been a King or Queen yet who's done one thing for the working population of this country. They're reactionaries, Tories to a man.

ALF: I know that, but they've no power now. They're just bloody figureheads, that's all.

SID: Yes! But they're figureheads of a society that's based on class and inherited wealth and privilege. And we din't bring the Tory government down in '72 and '74, like we did, just to have one of them buggers parading up and down our pit yard and everybody bowing and scraping to him.

ALF: Look, brother, why don't you put yourself up for the union? Just don't rattle at the sidelines; any silly bugger can do that.

[SID *is shouting by now*]

SID: I might just do that and if I do it'll be your job I shall put up for.

[*The* STEWARD *of the club crosses to the tables*]

STEWARD: That's all there is, ladies and gentlemen. Time's up. Can I have your glasses, please. Nice and sharply if you don't mind.

RONNIE: Oh, give over, Stan, not yet surely!

STEWARD: 'Fraid so, Ronnie, it's passed time if you must know. And when you see that rain coming down outside you'll want to get home pretty sharpish I bet.

DICK: It's not raining, is it?

STEWARD: It's coming down in sheets.

DICK: I'm off then.

[DICK *and* ALF *leave immediately. The others get up and look outside*]

ALBERT: Oh, my God, look at this lot.

RONNIE: Oh, bleeding hell. That's all we needed.

ALBERT: Oh, we're not going in this, are we?

RONNIE: We'll get wet through before we've gone ten yards.

SID: Where are we going to find two types of every animal known to man at this time of night?

ALBERT: Well, we can't stand here all night, can we?

SID: Go and get our lass's umbrella from our house, Ronnie.

[*They laugh*]

RONNIE: You'd only get two of us under that anyway.

[RONNIE *goes off*]

ALBERT: Where's he gone now?

[RONNIE *returns a few seconds later with one of the big striped umbrellas that fit over pub tables to act as sunshades*]

SID: Look at this silly bleeder. What's he got there?

RONNIE: I'll show you.

ALBERT: We're not going home under that bugger, are we?

[*They crowd under the umbrella*]

SID: Does the club know you've got it?

RONNIE: Ay, I'm going to take it back tomorrow. It'll be all right. Come on.

[*They move off, laughing and shouting. They pass a woman sheltering*]

WOMAN: Are you going anywhere near Princess Street?

RONNIE: No. But we can do. Get under.

ALBERT: Aye, come on.

WOMAN: I've just been to the hairdresser's.

SID: Were they shut?

[*The men all roar with laughter. They shout to other people to join them under the umbrella. 'Come on', 'come on'*]

General manager's office

The next day: it's still pouring with rain. FORBES *is staring out of the window. There is a knock on the door and* SHEILA *comes in*]

SHEILA: I've brought today's mail.

[FORBES *does not turn round or answer her*]

Is everything all right, Mr Forbes?

FORBES: Have you seen it, Sheila?

SHEILA: Seen what?

FORBES: The stack. Ruined. Bloody ruined.

[SHEILA *walks to the window and stands beside him, looking out*]

FORBES: The grass, the seed, the lot. All washed away.

SHEILA: Oo, what a shame.

FORBES: In about another week they'd have been strong enough to stand all this.

SHEILA: It's all this rain. This morning when we got up the

conservatory was like a swimming pool. It had come through the roof.

FORBES: I know, but it'd have looked like a big green hill, especially from a helicopter. You know, he'd have thought he'd have been landing in the Peak District instead of a pit yard.

SHEILA: Oh, it's a shame.

The pit head

SID, ALBERT, RONNIE *and* ALAN *have just finished a shift. As they leave the cage at the pit head they see a* MINER *fitting a pair of velvet curtains over a commemorative plaque on the wall.*

ALBERT: Hey, it's all right, in'it?

MINER: It's not finished yet.

RONNIE: What is it?

MINER: It's the plaque

ALBERT: Beautiful. What's it say?

   [SID *reads the plaque*]

SID: 'This plaque commemorates the visit of His Royal Highness the Prince of Wales to Milton Colliery, 14th June 1976.'

ALBERT: Beautiful. Beautiful.

ALAN: Hey up, I went into the office yesterday to see about the tax they owe me. Linda saw to me.

ALBERT: Which Linda's that?

ALAN: Big Linda.

ALBERT: Bristol's!

ALAN: Bristol's Linda.... They've had some pamphlets made for when Charlie comes. Little coloured booklets –

she showed me, she let me have a look at it.

ALBERT: She let you have a look at it, Linda did ... I bet you wish she had.

[*The men laugh*]

RONNIE: If Linda let you have a look you'd just throw your cap at it and run a mile.

ALAN: Would I?

RONNIE: You would.

ALAN: Hey, they haven't made a bad job of them booklets though, Sid.

[RONNIE *walks away a few yards*]

SID: What's it about?

ALAN: It's about the history of the pit and how they make coal and there's coloured pictures of the shaft in it and men working.

SID: I bet there isn't a picture of that in it.

ALBERT: What's that?

SID: Ronnie peeing.

[*The men laugh.* RONNIE *comes back zipping his trousers up*]

RONNIE: Hey up, what's going to happen if he wants to go when he's down the pit?

SID: Someone will have to tell him to hold it, won't they?

ALBERT: That's the only thing they've forgotten. They've done everything but that. They haven't put any toilets in down there.

ALAN: You talk stupid. How can you have flush lavs down a pit?

ALBERT: Who's talking about flush lavs? I'm on about them chemical jobs. Have you heard of them? They call them elsans. They had them on Lancaster bombers during the war when they were bombing Germany. They have them on showgrounds now. Tell you what, though, if they get them for him, they'll have to go on top of the winding gear.

RONNIE: Why?

ALBERT: Because they tell me he's the highest peer in the realm.

[KEN TAYLOR, *the deputy, walks up behind them*]

KEN: Now then, what you bloody lot looking at here?

ALBERT: We're waiting for the Punch and Judy show to start.

KEN: Now listen, here fellas, I'm hoping that you've all read them notices in the pit baths ... about swearing. You know there's a royal visit coming off and that's what it's been put up for.

SID: Well you can depend on us, Ken, lad, because we wouldn't want him to go home thinking that anybody swore down there, would we?

KEN: So we don't want no effing and blinding, or foul-mouthed language like that.

[*The men put on posh voices*]

ALBERT: Listen here, old boy, but I do believe I hear the cage approaching ... we must go thither....

SID: Yes, I must go home to my house now.

RONNIE: I'm playing polo tonight.

KEN: Go on, bugger off home. Get off, all of you ... sling your bloody hook.

RONNIE: No swearing; remember, Ken.

KEN: And don't be late tomorrow!

Sid's house

It is the night before the royal visit.

SID: Come on, son, let's have you in bed now.

MARK: Oh, dad.

SID: Come on, get off to bed. If you're not in bed when your mum comes home I shall cop it.

MARK: There's some kids in our class don't go to bed 'til ten.

SID: Some of the kids in your class tell lies as well.... Come on.

MARK: Dad?

SID: What?

MARK: I don't want to go to the pit to watch tomorrow. I want to go fishing.

SID: What's your mum say about it?

MARK: I don't know, I've not asked her.

SID: Well they've given you the day off for the visit, you know, not to go fishing.

MARK: They haven't. Not really. Just gave us the day off because royalty were coming. We don't get royalty every day.

SID: You're expected to go, though, aren't you?

MARK: No, not really. Stacks of kids....

SID: Look, I don't want all your school stood outside them gates cheering and you walking down the road in the opposite direction with your fishing rod on your back to the reservoir.

MARK: Them kids that are there will be the little la-di-das. All the rest of them are either going playing football or ice-skating. That's what Phil Fletcher and Jason ... they're going ice-skating.

SID: You're not kidding me? Because you always start stammering when you're having me on.

MARK: I'm not, honest. Cross me heart and hope to die.

SID: If you're kidding me I'll tan your backside, you know.

MARK: I'm not!

[SID *looks at him hard*]

SID: I'll see what your mam says, anyway, when she comes in.

MARK: No, don't!

SID: Why not?

MARK: Because she'll make me go with her and our Janet.

SID: No, she'll not. Not if what you're saying is right, she won't.

MARK: It is right.

SID: Well, you're old enough to make your own mind up about it. Anyway, come on, let's have you off to bed or else you'll be too tired to do anything in the morning.

[MARK *gets his comics from under the cushion and makes his way towards the stairs*]

MARK: Dad, why haven't you got the day off tomorrow?

SID: Somebody's got to run pit, haven't they? If we had the day off there'd be nobody there. That's the whole idea of the visit, isn't it, so that he gets an idea of what goes off.

MARK: You think it's daft this, don't you, this visit?

SID: I'm not too keen on it.

MARK: No, I know. Why aren't you so keen on it?

SID: I don't see what all this fuss and palaver's about, that's all.

MARK: But he's important, in't he?

SID: Aye, he's important all right.

[*He laughs*]

MARK: What're you laughing at? There's nothing funny there.

SID: It's like this, you see. Now, you go down to that reservoir, don't you, and you go fishing there. And some days you'll sit there all day and never catch a thing. Let's say he wants to go fishing. He says tomorrow I fancy a bit of fishing. They'll stock that reservoir up, won't they? There'll be perch and tench and roach. There'll be all sorts in it. Well, I don't think that's right, see. Them fish should be in there for them people that fish there regular. They're the people who've got a right to 'em. Do you see what I'm trying to get at?

[MARK *nods his head then walks across the room to the door*]

MARK: Ah well, I'll be off then. 'Night.

SID: What's them comics for?

MARK: Put by my bed for tomorrow.

SID: I'll be up in five minutes you know to check – that light had better be off.... And don't forget to clean your teeth either.

MARK: No ... 'night ... see you ... 'night.

General manager's office

Early morning. FORBES *is speaking on the phone.*

FORBES: Hello. Yes. Quickly, get me Bob Richards. [*Pause*] Have you seen it? On the wall next to the gate. Two foot letters that's all. About Scargill. 'Scargill Rules. OK'. Have you seen it?... Well, get it cleaned up or we're going to be the laughing stock of the bloody pit.... Get somebody up there and get it painted over.... No, better still, go up there yourself, make sure he does it, then check round, because if I ever find that thick-headed sod what's done that I'll string the bastard up, I will.

The pit yard 5

In the pit yard the two men from the bomb squad have arrived. One of them notices an old army knapsack in a corner.

BS 1: What's that?

CARTER: That? Oh, it's somebody's snap bag.

BS 1: What do you think?

[*The* BOMB SQUAD MEN *have a closer look*]

BS 2: We'd better check it.

BS 1: [*To* CARTER] Whose is it?

CARTER: I don't know. But I can find out if you like.

[*He looks round and shouts to a man working nearby*]

CARTER: Geoff! Come here, I want you. Whose is this snap bag here?

GEOFF: That's Alec Hemsley's, why?

CARTER: [*To* BOMB SQUAD MEN] Do you want us to get him?

BS 1: If you would, please.

CARTER: [*To* GEOFF] Where's he working?

GEOFF: He's working in the shop over there.

CARTER: Go and get him then, bring him here. And tell him to be quick.

BS 1: Funny place to leave a snap bag, all the same.

[ALEC *arrives back with* GEOFF]

CARTER: Alec, is this your snap bag here?

ALEC: It is.

CARTER: Well, these two gentlemen are from the bomb squad and they're just checking to make sure there's no bombs been planted round about, for the visit, you know.

ALEC: Oh aye. Well, I always leave it there.

CARTER: You always leave it there, do you?

ALEC: Aye, always.

BS 1: Would you open it up, please?

ALEC: Well, I can tell you what the contents are without opening it.

CARTER: No, you'd best do as they say, Alec, because they can't take any chances, you know, in their game.

ALEC: Oh, all right.

[ALEC *walks over and picks up his bag*]

Well, aren't we all right here? One flask, one paper, one snap tin, [*Opening a sandwich*] one sandwich with jam in it. Satisfied?

BS 1: Yes, thanks very much. You can put them all away now. Sorry to have troubled you.

ALEC: All right, no bother. [*Pause*] Listen, if the missus wanted to get rid of me she wouldn't bother with no bomb. It'd be the bread knife straight in the middle of the back.

The pit yard 6

In response to FORBES*'s telephone call,* BOB RICHARDS *leads two* APPRENTICES *round to the offending wall.*

RICHARDS: You've got to get it done this morning. It's got to be finished.

FIRST APPRENTICE: Hey, it's great ... it looks all right, that, don't it?

RICHARDS: Bloody terrible.

SECOND APPRENTICE: We ought to leave it up.

RICHARDS: No, I'll tell you what I want. I want the whole wall painting.

FIRST APPRENTICE: The whole wall?

[*The* APPRENTICES *are not pleased.* BOB RICHARDS *leaves them to it*]

The telephone office

In the pit yard BOB RICHARDS *is having a last-minute inspection. He passes the telephone office. The window frame has been freshly painted and a housebrick has been stood on end on the window sill to hold the bottom window up.* BOB RICHARDS *notices it, stops and looks through the window.* TOM, *the telephonist, is sitting at a switchboard and another office worker,* STAN, *is with him.* BOB RICHARDS *bends down to talk to* TOM.

RICHARDS: 'Ere! You'll have to shift this brick from here, Tom.

TOM: What for?

RICHARDS: Well, it's an eyesore stuck there, isn't it?

TOM: Well, it's been an eyesore for the last eighteen months, then, and nobody's complained 'til now.

RICHARDS: I haven't got time to argue. You know exactly what I mean, now get it shifted, will you?

TOM: The only way that brick's getting shifted is if you get that joiner down and get that sash mended. Then it'll stay open on its own. It gets like an oven in here.

STAN: We're sweating like pigs as it is.

TOM: There's no air in the place at all.

[BOB RICHARDS *tries to pull the top window down, but it is stuck*]

TOM: You won't move it.

RICHARDS: Well, we haven't got time to fetch the joiner down, have we?

TOM: Well, it's stopping then.

RICHARDS: I'll go and fetch the manager down, shall I?

TOM: You can bring anyone you like down. If that brick goes, we're straight out through that door.

General manager's office

SHEILA *and* LINDA *enter with two small packages*.

LINDA: Where have you got to put them?

SHEILA: In the Staff Changing Room.

LINDA: How did you know what kind of soap to get?

SHEILA: I picked out one that said 'By appointment'. Look.

LINDA: Oh yes.

SHEILA: The shampoo is as well. Can you see, at the bottom?

[LINDA *looks at the bottle and reads it*]

LINDA: Oh yes. 'By appointment to Her Majesty the Queen'.... Good idea, that. I'd have never thought of it. Do you think he'll want to wash his hair, then?

SHEILA: Oh, I should think so. Yes. When he's been down the pit.

LINDA. Oh, I'd better get his boots ready.

[LINDA *starts unpacking his new boots*]

LINDA: Takes the same size as our Derek, he does.

SHEILA: Does he?

LINDA: Yes, look.

SHEILA: Oh, hasn't he got big feet?

LINDA: Yes, our Derek has.

SHEILA: You know what they say about people with big feet don't you . . . ?

[*They both start to giggle*]

The telephone office

PETE, *the apprentice, walks up to the outside of the telephone office. He calls to the men through the window.*

PETE: The foreman tells me there's a brick round here. Is it right?

TOM: Aye, what you going to do with it?

PETE: Paint it.

[TOM *and* STAN *laugh*]

TOM: Paint the brick?

PETE: Aye.

TOM: Whose idea's that?

PETE: Bob's.

TOM: You're not having me on are you?

PETE: No. Where's the brick?

TOM: That's the only one we've got round here. He's going round the bend. He must be.

[PETE *sets to work with the paintbrush*]

STAN: He's painting it an' all.

TOM: You're not painting it, are you?

PETE: Aye.

TOM: Does the management know about this?

PETE: Aye, I'm under direct managerial instructions.

THE ARRIVAL

The pit yard

A line of school children led by a TEACHER *enter the pit yard.*

TEACHER: Now, I'm going to give you a flag each. Now, I don't want you messing about or waving them. When the helicopter comes, that will be the time to wave them. All right? I'll give the signal and you'll wave. Right, come on, let's go and get lined up in our place, there's not much time left. Come on, keep in line.

General manager's office

FORBES *and* MRS FORBES *are in the office getting ready. She is putting a flower into his lapel.*

FORBES: Come on, love, hurry up, we ought to be out there now.

MRS FORBES: Don't get aeriated, Stan. We'll be out there in a minute.

FORBES: Yes, but I ought to check everything's all right.

MRS FORBES: Well, off you go, then, I've done now.

The ripping edge

SID, ALBERT, RONNIE *and* ALAN *are hard at work in the mine.*

General manager's office

SHEILA *and* LINDA *come in and quickly take it in turns to look in the mirror on the wall to adjust their hair. They rush out then into the yard.*

The pit yard

The men are looking at their watches. FORBES *and* MRS FORBES *join them. A helicopter is heard approaching.*

FORBES: Everything all right? Right! Here it comes, there it is. Right, come on, he's arriving.

[*The group moves off to meet HRH*]

The reservoir

MARK *is sitting fishing. We hear the cheers and crowd noises of the pit yard. A brass band plays the national anthem. Throughout it all* MARK *continues fishing.*

Back to Reality

Cast

(*in order of appearance*)

MARK, nine-year-old son of Sid and Kath
TONY, elder son of Sid and Kath
SID STOREY, a miner
KATH STOREY, Sid's wife
FORBES, the pit general manager
SHEILA, Forbes's secretary
SID, a miner, leader of a team of rippers
ALBERT, a miner
RONNIE KING, a miner
ALAN DOBSON, trainee miner
HARRY, a miner
FRANK MORRIS, electrician
STEVE OATES, apprentice electrician
KEN TAYLOR, pit deputy
STAN, a miner
GEORGE, a miner
MRS ROBINSON, wife of Doncaster rescue team member
JOE ⎫
ROY ⎪
ERIC ⎬ miners
JIMMY ⎭
WILF, pit deputy
CAPTAIN OF RESCUE TEAM
ALF MEAKIN, NUM branch secretary

CARTER, pit deputy manager
BEATSON, under manager
AN OVERMAN
MRS KING, Ronnie's wife
MRS DOBSON, Alan's mother
MR DOBSON, Alan's father
JANET, Sid and Kath's schoolgirl daughter
DAVID, member of Doncaster rescue team
REPORTER
ACKROYD, NUM official
BANKSMAN
MR OATES, the apprentice's father
MRS OATES, the apprentice's mother
MR JOHNSON, the local MP
RESCUER 1
RESCUER 2
MAURICE, a young rescuer
SALVATION ARMY WOMAN
RESCUER 3
RESCUER 4
Other RESCUERS, REPORTERS

Back to Reality

ACT ONE

1: The back yard

TONY *and* MARK *are playing cricket in the yard at the back of their house. The stumps and wickets are chalked on the wall.* TONY *is batting. You can tell by the way he holds the bat that he has played before. He plays the next ball easily back to the bowler.* MARK *bowls again.* TONY, *perhaps a little too relaxed because the bowler is only nine years old, is beaten by it.* MARK *jumps up with his arms outstretched.*

MARK: Out!

TONY: Was it heck.

MARK: Course it was. It hit the off-stump.

TONY: Talk sense. It was a mile wide.

[MARK *inspects the ball*]

MARK: See! I told you: there's chalk on it. Look.

TONY: Where? . . . Ar, one speck. You need a magnifying glass to see it an' all.

MARK: It don't matter. It's still out.

[TONY *hands him the bat*]

TONY: It wouldn't have knocked the bails off, though.

MARK: As though it could. It'd take a cannon ball to knock them bails off.

TONY: I mean in a real match, you fool.

[TONY *walks back to the bowling mark, then carries on walking towards the far end of the yard, polishing the worn tennis ball on his jeans*]

TONY: You can get ready now, lad.

[*He pretends to look ferocious and starts to growl*]

MARK: Give over, Tony. If I slog out at it and it goes through somebody's window, it's not my fault.

[*With a roar,* TONY *sets off, sprints up to the bowling mark and, instead of bowling the fastest ball of all time, he bowls a high, slow full toss. Totally confused,* MARK *swings at it, misses, and the ball drops on to the wicket.* TONY *is too amused to even shout 'Out'*]

MARK: Not out! Not out!

TONY: Course it was out. It hit the wicket, didn't it?

MARK: I know, but it wasn't fair.

TONY: Why wasn't it?

MARK: Cos it wasn't, that's why!

[TONY *is still teasing him, and* MARK *chases him round the yard.* TONY *finds this even funnier. Then* SID *comes out of the house*]

SID: Now then. What's going off?

MARK: It's him. He's messing about. He won't bowl right.

TONY: I was only having a bit of fun with him.

SID: Fun. You don't have fun when you play at cricket. Cricket's a serious business.

MARK: He reckoned to bowl as fast as he could, then he sent a right high one that I couldn't hit.

SID: Bowlers don't bowl 'em for batsmen to hit. Now, get in and let's have a look at you.

[SID *throws the ball to* TONY]

SID: On a length, but not too fast for him.

> [SID *looks at* MARK's *stance. Even at his age it is obvious that he has been coached*]

Left   shoulder   pointing   down   the   wicket,
Mark. . . . That's it. And if I see you slogging out at the
first ball, I'll tan your arse for you. Play yourself in first.

> [TONY *bowls.* MARK *plays a forward defensive shot, safely and correctly.* SID , crouching at mid-off, fields the ball]

Well played. Get your left foot right out to the ball, and
your head over it.

> [KATH *comes out of the back door with the 'snap' for* TONY *and* SID. *They both go over to collect it, and put it into the pockets of their jackets.* KATH *tells them it's late*]

MARK: If we win tonight we're playing the final at Shaw
Lane at Barnsley.

SID: If I'd known it was the semi-final you were playing
in, I'd have swapped a shift and come and watched you.

TONY: Who are you playing? King Street?

MARK: Market Street.

TONY: I once took eight for seven against them. They were
all out for sixteen . . . and five of them were byes.

MARK: I bet you wouldn't have got me out.

TONY: You what?

SID: He would. He'd have got anybody out that day. Even
you.

> [*The two men have their jackets on, ready for work. Then* SID *remembers something, and takes an envelope out of his pocket and gives it to* MARK]

SID: Oh, I nearly forgot. I've got something for you, Mark.

MARK: What is it?

[MARK *tears open the envelope, and finds two tickets inside. He reads them*]

MARK: Oo! They're for the Test Match. At Headingley. Great! When is it? ... Saturday the twenty-sixth ... When's that?

SID: A week on Saturday.

MARK: Great! Did my uncle Harry get them for you?

SID: Yes.

MARK: We might be on tele, eh?

SID: Come on, Tony, let's get cracking or else they'll be starting without us.

TONY: Ta-ra, mam. I'm going straight round to Linda's after work. I'll see you later.

KATH: Ta-ra, love.

[SID *kisses* KATH *on the cheek*]

SID: Ta-ra, love.

KATH: See you tonight.

SID: [*To* MARK] And don't forget. Get your head down the first few overs. Don't be going mad.

[*The men leave and* MARK *is left reading the tickets again, turning them over and enjoying them*]

2: The general manager's office

In his office, FORBES, *the general manager, is sitting at his desk phoning.*

FORBES: Tom? This is Forbes. Get me Ken Taylor, will you?

[*There is a knock on the door, and* SHEILA, *his secretary, comes in with his coffee. She places it on his desk, and turns to go*]

Wait a minute, love. I want you.

[*She waits for him to finish*]

FORBES: Hello, Ken? Did they get that motor mended on Fourteen's face this morning? ... Bloody hell! Get it seen to, will you, Ken? I thought they said they'd get it done.... Well, listen. I want the bugger seen to first thing. If we're not careful, we're going to lose two full shifts on that face ... I know ... I know. I know you are, Ken.... No, I never said that Ken. I never said you were messing about. All I said was that I wanted it seeing to this afternoon.... All right then, Ken. Do your best. Cheerio.

[*He puts the phone down*]

Sorry about that, love, but you can't help but swear sometimes.

[*He reaches into his 'out' tray and sorts out some papers to give her*]

SHEILA: I'm used to it by now, I should be. I've heard you often enough, haven't I?

FORBES: I can see what's going to happen now. There'll be two shifts lost. Production will be down. They'll look at the figures at area and get straight on the phone. Then when you try to explain they just think you're making excuses....

[*He has a drink of coffee*]

Anyway, that'll be next week. I'll face that problem when it comes.

3: The pit locker room

SID *and the other three rippers in his team,* ALBERT, RONNIE *and the trainee,* ALAN, *are in the 'dirty' side putting on their pit clothes. Two or three other miners, including* HARRY, *are also changing.* SID *takes out a pair of green and white football socks. As soon as he starts to pull them on the others notice them.*

HARRY: Bloody hell, they're bobby dazzlers, aren't they, Sid?

SID: I'm thinking of making a comeback. I'm going to get back into training.

HARRY: Get back into bed, you mean.

ALAN: They could do with you down at Sheffield you know ... they need some new players – both teams.

SID: Don't you worry about me, lad. I can still do it if I want to.

[SID *starts to do a few loosening up exercises, trying to touch his toes and throwing his arms back. The men are joking amongst themselves*]

ALBERT: Give over, Sid, it's wearing me out just watching you.

HARRY: Aye, give over, Sid.

[TONY *walks past the end of the bay. He is wearing pit clothes, ready to go down. Then he sees his dad wearing his football socks*]

TONY: Hey up, what you doing with them socks on? They're mine.

SID: Well you weren't using them, were you? They've been stuck in that drawer since you left school. Somebody might as well get some use out of them.

TONY: What if I want them, though?

SID: What are you going to want them for?

TONY: Well, I might start playing again.

SID: There's only one thing you're interested in playing with and it's not football.

[*The others laugh.* TONY *walks away, not too pleased*]

ALAN: He was a good footballer at school, your Tony.

HARRY: He was a better cricketer.

SID: He's only interested in one wicket and that's his middle'un. He's too busy courting, that's his trouble.

[*The men laugh amongst themselves*]

4: The general manager's office

FORBES *is talking on the phone*.

FORBES: ... I know, Ken, but you know how it is. I just wanted to know what's happening ... Yes ... Well that's OK then ... I'll leave you to it. If we lose production and they get to know the figures at area office the phone will never stop ringing ... No, I'm not asking you to rush it, Ken ... No ... I just don't want to have to start making excuses. So keep me in touch, OK? ... Right. Any problems – let me know.

[*He puts the phone down*]

5: Underground

SID, ALBERT, RONNIE *and* ALAN *are walking to work underground. They reach two men sitting at a junction:* FRANK, *the electrician, and* STEVE, *the apprentice*.

SID: You've got a good job, haven't you? What are you doing sat here?

ALBERT: They look like Butch Cassidy and the Sundance Kid, don't they?

SID: They look like a couple of hitch-hikers to me.

RONNIE: They'll wait a long time for a lift there.

SID: They'll get a lift up the arse if the deputy sees them.

FRANK: We're waiting to go on Fourteen's to mend that motor on the conveyor.

RONNIE: Hey, never. Haven't they got that bugger fixed yet?

FRANK: No, not yet. Day shift made a start on it.

RONNIE: I was going to say, the day shift were supposed to be seeing to it.

FRANK: They started it but they didn't get it done. We're waiting for some pull lifts to be sent down from the pit top. Ken Taylor's seeing to it. We can't do any more until we get some lifting tackle on the job.

SID: Well, while you're waiting you can come with us and mend our television.

STEVE: What television?

SID: We've got a portable tele in the gate. Forbes says we can only have it on at snaptime though. He says we'll not do the job right if we watch it while we're working.

STEVE: I wouldn't have thought a tele would have worked down here. Too much static.

SID: It's a good one, is this. A Japanese set.

FRANK: Colour, Sid?

SID: Definitely.

FRANK: We'll get it mended then. There's racing on from Thirsk this afternoon. What's up with it?

SID: I don't know. I think a valve might have gone.

FRANK: Right. I'll get on the blower to the stores and ask 'em to send one down.

STEVE: I didn't know they stocked television valves in the stores. I've never seen any.

[*The rippers walk away up the gate, laughing. The penny drops for* STEVE]

You're taking the piss out of me, aren't you?

[FRANK *takes out his racing form book and studies it with his cap lamp*]

Don't you ever get sick and tired of studying that thing, Frank?

FRANK: Course I don't. There's a mine of information in here. It's going to win me a fortune one day.

STEVE: Aye, but it's only mugs who back horses. My dad says he's never seen a poor bookie.

FRANK: I suppose he's right, but if you're going to bet 10p each way or 20p each way, you're never going to make any money, are you. What you need, you see, you've got to work a system out.

STEVE: Have you got a good system.

FRANK: I've got a good system.

STEVE: Can't be all that good.

FRANK: Why's that?

STEVE: Well, you're still working down here with me, aren't you?

FRANK: That's because I haven't got any capital to start with. You've got to invest some money in it, see, before you can get any out, haven't you?

STEVE: I suppose so. You should be on 'Mastermind', Frank, all that stuff you know about horses.

[KEN TAYLOR *walks up the roadway towards them. When they see who it is they stand up and* FRANK *puts his book away inside his overalls*]

KEN: Now then Frank, have you found any?

FRANK: Not a thing. Nothing at all.

KEN: Bloody hellfire. Anyway, come on, let's go down here and see if we can find any. What a bleeding pantomime this is, I don't know.

[*They start to walk up the roadway*]

STEVE: What's up with you? I'm not bothered. I could do this all shift. While you're marching, you're not fighting, that's what my dad says.

KEN: We're walking about like second-hand arseholes and we're not getting anything done, are we? . . . Forbes is playing hell with me on this job down here. Anyway, Frank, when you get started, I wonder if you could repair that bagging on the pump. I mean, we may as well do it while the face is stood, mightn't we?

FRANK: I'll have a look at it, Ken.

KEN: Right. Do your best, then, won't you?

[*He goes off as* FRANK *and* STEVE *start work*]

FRANK: Now just tighten these nuts up, Steve, will you?

STEVE: Like this?

FRANK: Yes, that's it.

[*They work together for a while*]

I'm going to leave you to finish this cowl, Steve, while I go and attend to that bagging that Ken was on about in the gate. All right.

STEVE: Yes.

FRANK: Don't dawdle, because you know we're in a hurry.

STEVE: Switch the power on when I give you a shout, won't you, Frank?

FRANK: All right.

[FRANK *goes off to mend the pump in the gate.* STEVE *continues to work alone for quite a while*]

STEVE: [*To himself*] Right then, just do this and that should be it.

6: The ripping edge

SID's *team is working at the ripping edge. They have just cleared the ripping and are ready to set a ring.*

RONNIE: Go on, Albert, that'll do it, son. Go on, I've got it.

[ALAN *and* SID *walk up the gate to fetch a ring.* ALBERT *and* RONNIE *stay at the ripping edge*]

ALBERT: And don't be long about it.

[*There is a blue flash and a blast of air so strong that it knocks men flying. Then darkness and the noise of the roof falling in. There is complete chaos. Those on the three-foot-high coal face are crawling along as fast as they are able. Others, with a little more room, are running away from the direction of the explosion. There is much shouting and confusion*]

7: The telephone calls

a) *Coal conveyor transfer point*

The force of the explosion has knocked HARRY *to the floor. His helmet has been blown off and he has cut his head. He feels at his head, looks at the blood on his fingers, then picks his helmet up and puts it back on. He is dazed. The air is still thick with dust and he is coughing and choking all the time. He moves painfully to the telephone and shouts into it.*

HARRY: Hello! Hello! ... [*There is no answer*] ... Hello! Hello! There's been an explosion on Fourteen's!

[*There is still no reply. The explosion has put the telephone system out of order.* STAN *and* GEORGE *enter*]

GEORGE: Is that Harry?

HARRY: George? Who's that with you?

GEORGE: Stan Walker.

STAN: What's happened, Harry?

HARRY: There must have been an explosion somewhere.

STAN: I can smell smoke, there must be a fire somewhere.

HARRY: We're going to have to find a phone and let 'em know on the pit top.

GEORGE: This dust's killing me. I can't breathe.

STAN: I'm going to put my self-rescuer on, see if that improves things.

[*All three men unfasten their self-rescuers – their breathing apparatus – from their belts and start to put them on*]

HARRY: Listen, we've got to keep together and not panic. Who's going first?

STAN: I'll go first.

HARRY: My bloody head's killing me.

GEORGE: Come on then, let's get cracking.

[*They fix their nose clips on, put their mouthpieces in and set off in single file up the gate. The dust is so thick that it almost nullifies the beams of their lamps. They can barely see each other and they are feeling their way along rather than seeing their way*]

b) *General manager's office*

FORBES *is standing, answering the telephone.*

FORBES: Right, Tom. Emergency procedure straight into

operation. Phone Doncaster Rescue Station straightaway, then Rotherham and Wakefield. I want the whole pit cleared and the men checked out. Keep me informed.

[*He pushes down the telephone rest to clear the line, then starts to dial*]

c) *A council house*

MRS ROBINSON *has just picked up the telephone to answer it.*

MRS ROBINSON: Hello.... At Milton [*She shouts to her husband who is in the garden*] Cliff, it's Doncaster Rescue Station, there's been an accident at the pit. They want you. [*She goes back to the telephone*]. He's just getting his jacket. It's bloody marvellous, this. It takes me two months to get him to cut the front grass and as soon as he gets started you have to ring because something's happened at the pit.

8: The pit yard

The pit is being emptied. Some miners are helping HARRY, *who has just stepped out of the cage.*

JOE: Come on, let's get him across to the ambulance room.

HARRY: I'll be all right, what's up with you? I don't want to go to the ambulance room.

ROY: You'll have to get your head seen to, Harry. Anyway, you'll have to report it just in case there's any repercussions afterwards. It's always best to cover yourself in these cases.

JOE: I think you ought to go to hospital Harry, for a check-up.

HARRY: I'll be all right.

ROY: You'll not. You need a couple of stitches in this for a start.

HARRY: I'm not going anywhere 'til I know what's happened to them lads in that heading.

[*They pass* TONY, JIMMY *and* ERIC]

JIMMY: I wondered what the bloody hell had happened. I was riding on the belt, then there was this thump and this terrific rush of air and everything went black. You couldn't see a thing. I thought I was a gonner, I can tell you. I thought my lamp had gone out 'til I held it to my hand. Then I realized it was the dust – it was that thick it had just blotted the beam out completely. I mean, you can't believe it, can you? Does anybody know where it's happened yet?

ROY: Somebody said it was on Fourteen's

ERIC: Is there anybody working in there?

JOE: There shouldn't be. What about Seventeen's, that's next door?

TONY: My dad's team's working in the tail-gate ...

[*The others look at each other without saying anything*]

... that doesn't mean that anything's happened to them, does it?

JIMMY: Look, it's no good jumping to conclusions. Nobody knows what's happened yet.

JOE: I'm not saying anything's happened to 'em. I'm just saying Seventeen is next door, that's all.

ERIC: Look, we don't know for definite whether it is on Fourteen's or not.

[JOE *and* ROY *leave*]

TONY: He's right, though, you know. He's not come up, my

dad. I haven't seen any of his mates either.

JIMMY: They're not all out yet. Perhaps they'll be on a later draw.

ERIC: Don't start panicking Tony. Wait and see.

TONY: I know, but what about my mother?

JIMMY: It's too early to be thinking about that yet. Wait until we know something definite first.

TONY: Somebody will tell her, though, won't they? Word will get round.

ERIC: Just wait a bit longer and let's get to know what's happened. It's no good frightening folks unnecessarily. Come on, Jimmy.

[*They go off as* WILF, *a pit deputy enters*]

TONY: Is there anybody still down there, Wilf?

WILF: I'm just off to the deployment centre to find out.

TONY: I mean, is there another draw? Are there any more waiting to come up?

WILF: Not that I know of.

TONY: You haven't seen my dad, have you?

WILF: No, I haven't, lad.

TONY: I'm coming with you.

WILF: You can't. The manager's to know first.

TONY: Who can't? My dad's still down there, you know.

WILF: You don't know that for definite yet. Look, I think the best thing you can do, Tony, is to go to Mr Forbes's office and wait there. He'll let you know as soon as we've checked.

[*As the two men are about to walk away, they are passed by the Doncaster rescue team carrying their equipment*]

RESCUE TEAM CAPTAIN: Where's the rescue room?

WILF: I'm going that way, I'll show you.

CAPTAIN: Any idea what's happened?

> [*The rescue team follow* WILF *as* TONY *goes the other way*]

9: The general manager's office

All the management team – FORBES, CARTER and BEATSON – are in the room, plus ALF MEAKIN, the union branch secretary, and SHEILA, FORBES's secretary. They are all quiet, watching FORBES who is on the telephone taking down the names of the missing men]

FORBES: Who? ... Is that the lot? ... Right, Tom, keep me informed.

> [*He puts the phone down*]

BEATSON: How many?

> [FORBES *counts the list*]

FORBES: Eight.

ALF: Who are they?

FORBES: There's Sid Storey's team – that's Sid, Albert Rhodes, Ronnie King and young Alan Dobson. Then there's Ken Taylor, Frank Morris, Steve Oates and George Kay.

> [FORBES *spreads out a surveyor's map on his desk showing the seam where the explosion has happened and the districts on that seam. The men crowd round the desk*]

ALF: This is where Sid's team's working, isn't it, Seventeen's tail-gate?

CARTER: What about the others, though? What are they doing in that district?

ALF: They're not forced to be where Sid's lot are, though, are they?

FORBES: We'd better get the deputy up. He should know what they were doing.

SHEILA: Mr Forbes, Tony Storey's outside. What shall I tell him?

[*The men have been so involved in the details and immediacy of the explosion that they have not yet thought about the problems of informing the relatives of the missing men*]

FORBES: I don't know. It seems a bit early to be telling anybody anything. Because they'll only think the worst.

ALF: We've got to tell them. As soon as the men get bathed and go home there'll be rumours all over the district. It's better that they're told properly than being kept in the dark; or told something that might be a pack of lies by the next-door neighbour.

CARTER: I agree with Alf. We've no right to withhold information at this stage.

FORBES: I'm not trying to withhold information. It's just the thought of frightening people unnecessarily, that's all. It's hard to know what to do for the best. . . . Phil, will you go round to the men's houses and inform their relatives?

BEATSON: What, on my own?

FORBES: No, Alf will go with you, won't you Alf? That will be the best plan. They'll know Alf better, anyway.

ALF: Yes, I'll go.

FORBES: Right, let's have Sid's lad in, then. He might want to tell his mother himself.

SHEILA: Come in, Tony.

TONY: Have you found anything yet?

FORBES: Well, as far as we can make out, there are still eight men unaccounted for. . . .

TONY: What about my dad?

FORBES: Yes, your dad's one of them. All the men in that heading are involved by the look of it.

TONY: [*Quietly, more to himself than anyone in the room*] Bloody hell!

FORBES: We don't know how bad the situation is just yet, though, Tony. The first rescue team have only just gone down. We won't know anything definite until they've reported.

TONY: How long will that be?

FORBES: It's impossible to tell. We don't know what conditions they're going to meet down there. We don't know if there's a fire, if there's been any falls, if there's gas still present. We shall just have to wait for them to report before we can determine the full seriousness of the incident.

ALF: Listen, Tony. We're going round to everybody's house who's involved in this, to let their wives know and that. Do you want to stop at the pit and let us tell your mother, or do you want to do it?

TONY: I don't know. I don't want to leave the pit in case I can do anything, but I think I ought to tell my mam.

ALF: Are you sure?

TONY: I'll tell her. I'll go home and then come back.

FORBES: I think that's a good idea. There's nothing anybody's going to be able to do here for a while anyway.

TONY: If there's going to be a list of volunteers, Alf, who might be needed to go down and help, I want to be on it.

ALF: I'll see to that, Tony.

FORBES: And tell your mother that if she wants to come down to the pit to await further information, Mr Beatson's room next door will be available for relatives.

TONY: OK.

[*He leaves the room. Nobody speaks for a few seconds*]

ALF: Well, Phil, we'd better get cracking.

BEATSON: Do you know where they all live, Alf?

ALF: Let's have a look.

[*He studies the list*]

ALF: I don't know where Frank Morris lives.

CARTER: He lives at Thorncliffe, doesn't he?

ALF: Anyway, we can get his address from the time office.

FORBES: Do you want to copy that list down?

ALF: No, I know who they are now.

BEATSON: Come on then, Alf, let's make a start.

ALF: Yes, let's get it over with. Christ Almighty, what a bloody job.

[*The two men leave the office*]

CARTER: I hope somebody's phoned the NUM offices at Barnsley and let them know.

FORBES: We did that straightaway, straight after we'd informed the Inspectorate.

CARTER: Thank God for that. That's all we needed, them storming in here complaining about being last to be told about it.

10: Sid's house

At home, KATH STOREY *does not hear* TONY *come in. He stands in the middle doorway and watches her working. Then she sees him, and the sight of him just standing there makes her jump.*

KATH: You dozy devil. You frightened me to death standing there. I wondered whoever it was. Anyway, what you doing home at this time? Are you on strike or something?

TONY: I wish we were. . . .

KATH: What do you mean? What you come home for?

TONY: There's been an accident. They've cleared the pit.

KATH: What sort of accident? Where's your dad?

TONY: I don't know. He hasn't come out. They've sent a rescue team down to find them.

KATH: What's happened, Tony? Tell me what's happened. Is he dead? Has he been killed?

TONY: Is he heck dead! I don't know what's happened. Nobody does yet. There's been an explosion and that's all we know until the rescue team makes a report.

[KATH *sits down in the armchair and holds her head in her hands.* TONY *just stands there, awkward*]

KATH: My God.

TONY: It'll be all right, mam. It's no good getting into a panic yet. Let's wait and see what's happened first. . . . I'm going back to the pit now, mam. I've put my name down just in case they need any help.

KATH: And what do you think I'm going to do, just sit here twiddling my thumbs? I'm coming with you.

TONY: What about our Janet and our Mark?

KATH: I'd better stop in until our Janet comes in, then tell her to wait for our Mark.

TONY: Make them stop at home, mam. It's no place for them down there.

KATH: Our Janet will want to come.

TONY: Well, tell her she can't. Tell her she's to stop in and look after our Mark. And tell her not to get all worked up and frighten him to death. Everything might be all right as far as we know. . . . When you get down to the offices they've set a room aside for relatives. It's Beatson's office. You'll see it.

[*She does not answer him. She does not appear to be listening*]

Do you want me to go and fetch my aunty Edna to come and wait with you?

KATH: No, our Janet will be home in a minute. It's nearly four o'clock.

TONY: Make yourself a cup of tea or something. Have I to put the kettle on for you?

KATH: No, you get off now. There's nothing you can do here.

TONY: I'll see you later, then.

[*He leaves*]

11: Underground

Doncaster Rescue Team are walking along the tail-gate. They are not wearing their breathing apparatus. The leading man is carrying a canary in a cage. They are being directed by one of the colliery overmen. They come to a massive fall which blocks the roadway and prevents any further progress. They stop and consider the fall with their lamps.

OVERMAN: We're going to need some help to shift that lot.

CAPTAIN: How far do you reckon it stretches back?

OVERMAN: There's no way of telling at this stage. I know one thing, though.

CAPTAIN: What?

OVERMAN: It must have been a hell of an explosion to bring that lot down.

CAPTAIN: Is there another way round?

OVERMAN: We'll have to go back up the main gate and see if we can get along the face. If we can get round that way.

CAPTAIN: How many men did you say are trapped in that gate? Five?

OVERMAN: Four, as far as we can make out.

[WILF, *the pit deputy, enters*]

WILF: There's water up that way.

CAPTAIN: Is there much?

WILF: Looks as though we could do with Sea-Link, if you ask me.

CAPTAIN: Jesus Christ!

WILF: I wish I was. I'd only have got the bottoms of my feet wet then.

OVERMAN: The explosion'll have knocked the pump out of action. What do you want to do? Go back up the return and round Twelve's, see if we can get in that way?

WILF: Well, the Wakefield Rescue Team are going into Twelve's. They're up to their waists in water. Having hell of a job keeping their equipment dry.

CAPTAIN: What about the Barnsley team?

WILF: They were just arriving as we came down.

OVERMAN: We'll be off then.

WILF: I'm going back to see if I can get through on the blower. I'm going to try and get somebody down to have a look at the pump. See if we can shift this lot.

CAPTAIN: Right. All the best.

[*The Doncaster Rescue Team go one way as* WILF *goes another*]

12: Beatson's office

The room already has some women waiting as at a doctor's surgery. ALF MEAKIN *is about to leave the office as* KATH *enters.*

ALF: Hello, Kath. Bloody bad job is this. I'd have come round but your Tony said he'd tell you.

KATH: Any news yet?

ALF: No, not yet.

KATH: What do you think, Alf?

ALF: I've no idea, love. We can't say. We don't know the extent of the explosion or anything. We'll just have to wait for the rescue teams to report. They'll be doing all they can, you can be assured of that.

KATH: Yes, I know they will.

ALF: Make yourself comfortable and as soon as there's any news you'll be informed. All right, love?

KATH: Yes. Thanks, Alf.

   [*He goes out*]

MRS KING: I can't believe it, Kath. I just can't believe it's happened.

KATH: We'll just have to hope for the best and hope that nothing has happened.

MRS KING: I just couldn't believe it when Alf told me. It wouldn't sink in. When I saw him I thought he'd brought me some eggs from the gardens. I buy a dozen off him every week.

MRS DOBSON: I was talking to Mrs Price. I knew there was something wrong as soon as I saw that other bloke with him.

13: Sid's house

JANET *is sitting looking through a magazine. She is too worked up to concentrate properly.*

MARK: [*Entering*] We won, mam. [*He looks around*]

JANET: She's not in.

MARK: She said she'd come to watch us. We won easy. They only got twenty-five. We passed that with only two wickets down.

JANET: She couldn't come. She told me to tell you.

MARK: Where is she? And my dad said he'd give me a penny for every run I got. I got eleven not out.

JANET: She's had to go down to the pit.

MARK: That's the second time in a row I've been not out now.... What's she gone down there for?

JANET: There's been an accident. Dad might be in it. She's gone to find out what's happened.

[MARK *starts to go out*]

MARK: I'm going to see.

JANET: You're not. My mam says you're to stop with me until she gets back.

MARK: I want to go.

JANET: You can't. If you go, Mark, you'll get into trouble. Dad will give you a good hiding when he gets home.... Now then, what do you want for your tea? There's some ravioli or some spaghetti hoops.

MARK: I don't want any tea. I'm going out.

JANET: Where are you going?

MARK: I'm going to play.

JANET: You'll be hungry. Come and have some tea, Mark, and tell me about the cricket match.

MARK: No. I'm going out.

JANET: Well, go down to the allotment and collect the eggs from the hen house then. And don't be long because my mam might be back at any time.

[*He goes out*]

14: Underground

The Doncaster rescue team is walking up Seventeen's main gate. The leader is carrying the canary in the cage. The canary starts to gasp a little, then to preen its feathers. These are signs of distress and the man holding the cage notices them immediately.

CAPTAIN: Hold it, there's gas here. Me and David'll investigate the face. I want the rest of you to wait until we get back.

[*The* CAPTAIN *of the team and the man nominated by him put on their breathing equipment and set off for the face. The canary stays with the remainder of the team. The two go off one way while the remainder of the team watch them leave*]

15: The allotments

MARK *is in the hen run, collecting the eggs from the nesting boxes. He arranges seven eggs in a cluster on the floor, then places them in a row and, crouching over them, he goes along the row pointing at each egg in turn.*

MARK: [*Quietly*] Yes – no – yes – no – yes – no – yes. [*He goes back to the beginning of the row and goes along it again. This time he begins differently*]. No – yes – no – yes – no – yes – no.

ACT TWO

16: Underground

The CAPTAIN *and the* OVERMAN *arrive back at the fresh air base on Seventeen's main gate. They meet the Doncaster rescue team, whom they had earlier left there.*

OVERMAN: What's it like?

CAPTAIN: Awful. The way into the face looks completely blocked. We're going to need all available rescue teams working from this end.

OVERMAN: Right, I'll get on the blower and we'll have some lads down to start clearing the tail-gate. There's no gas in there; that might be the quickest way in.

CAPTAIN: I want all surrounding colliery teams on standby on the surface. We're going to need a lot of men. They're going to be hampered for space up there, and they're not going to be able to work long at a stretch with their masks on.

[*The* OVERMAN *hurries away to the telephone*]

DAVID: It's a bad one, is this, Jack.

CAPTAIN: I know, but it's a lot worse for them poor buggers behind it.

[*They go off*]

17: The canteen

Men are standing around, smoking and drinking tea, talking about the incident. TONY *is standing with* JIMMY *and* ERIC.

ERIC: They've had trouble with gas in Fourteen's before, though, haven't they?

JIMMY: Who says it's on Fourteen's anyroad? We don't know where it is for definite.

ERIC: No, but it looks odds on, doesn't it, according to Alf? I suppose it could have been caused by a blow-out of gas from the old workings.

JIMMY: [*Sarcastically*] An act of God, lad, that's what it'll be.

ERIC: That's what they always try to make out, isn't it? More like somebody's slipped up somewhere. That's usually the case.

JIMMY: There's no wonder, is there, pressure that's put on us. If we went by the book we wouldn't get a spoonful of coal out a shift. Everybody knows that. In fact it's a wonder we get away with it as often as we do.

TONY: What gets me is all this hanging about. They must be sending some information up. We've a right to know, haven't we? Bloody hell, my dad's down there. I've a right to know what's going off.

[ALF MEAKIN *comes into the canteen*]

ALF: Listen, lads. There's been a fall in Seventeen's tail-gate and we want some volunteers to clear it.

[*There is a general movement towards the door.* ALF *has to shout above the noise of men moving and talking*]

ALF: You'll have to work in teams. Four to a team, I reckon. Any more and you'll be getting in each other's way. We'll work half-hour stints, then another lot take over.

[*A* REPORTER *with a notepad enters*]

REPORTER: Any news, Mr Meakin?

ALF: I've just heard that Boycott's a hundred and seventy-seven not out, if that's any use to you.

18: The general manager's office

FORBES, CARTER, BEATSON *and* ACKROYD, *an NUM official,
are in the room.* FORBES *is bringing the NUM official up to
date on the rescue operation. They are looking at the map
spread out on* FORBES'S *desk.*

FORBES: The Wakefield rescue team are searching Fourteen's. The Doncaster, Barnsley and other auxiliary
teams are trying to break through on this face here and
we've got a team of our lads tackling a fall in the tail-
gate here.

ACKROYD: What about fire?

FORBES: We've had no reports of fire burning anywhere.

ACKROYD: And gas?

FORBES: There's gas present in the main gate
here.... The men clearing that fall are having to use
oxygen.

ACKROYD: And you've no idea as to the cause of the explosion yet?

FORBES: None at all. All we've been concerned with so far
is getting the rescue operation into motion.

ACKROYD: I'd like to go down myself as soon as it's conve-
nient.

FORBES: That's all right.

CARTER: As long as we clear it with one of the rescue
teams.

FORBES: I can't see any problems there. Let's go and see.

  [FORBES *and* ACKROYD *leave. As they do so* ALF MEAKIN
  hurries in]

ALF: Look, I've got to see you about this quickly. Who's
put the press and TV people in the surveyor's office?

CARTER: I have. It's the best place for them. They can use
the drawing tables to work on. Why?

ALF: Why? They're a bloody nuisance, that's why. It's a wonder they haven't taken over the whole building and shoved us out into the yard.

BEATSON: They've their job to do, Alf, like everybody else. They need somewhere to do it from.

ALF: I wouldn't have them on the premises if it was anything to do with me. They're like bloody vultures, pestering you every time you make a move. If news came in that there was a bigger accident somewhere, a plane crash with two hundred killed, they'd pack their tackle up and be off like a shot. They don't care a bugger really. It's something to write about, that's all. . . .

CARTER: They've had strict instructions not to harass any of the relatives or they're out on their backsides.

ALF: Good. Does anybody know if any tea's been sent in for them?

BEATSON: I think Sheila's seeing to it.

ALF: I'll just go and check, see if they're all right.

[ALF *leaves*]

BEATSON: Old Alf's on his high horse, isn't he?

CARTER: There's some truth in what he says, though. They'll milk the last drop out of it. I can see the headlines already. 'Disaster strikes at royal visit pit'. And folks will say, it's a good job he went a month back and not yesterday.

19: Beatson's office

A man dressed in a boiler suit and a jacket over the top of it comes into the room. It is MR OATES, *the apprentice electrician's father. His face is dirty. He has come straight from work. He goes straight across to his wife, who is sitting in one of the chairs.*

MR OATES: Why didn't you let me know? Why didn't you ring me or something?

MRS OATES: I didn't want to frighten you. I thought we'd have known something by now. I wanted to know something definite first.

MR OATES: Frighten me! It frightens you when somebody hears it on the news, then comes and tells you when you're having your snap.

MRS OATES: Have you been to see the manager?

MR OATES: I've seen the under manager.

MRS OATES: Is there any news? Cos they're telling us nothing in here.

MR OATES: Nothing definite yet.

[ALF *comes in carrying a tray full of cups of tea and coffee.* SHEILA *follows him with a tray of sandwiches*]

ALF: Here we are, compliments of the Salvation Army.

SHEILA: Can you come and help yourselves, please? There's tea or coffee, and plenty of sandwiches if you'd like one.

[*Some of the people in the room start to take a drink.* ALF *takes a cup over to* KATH. MRS OATES *picks up two cups and moves back to her chair. She hands one of the cups to her husband*]

MRS OATES: Do you want a sandwich?

MR OATES: No, I couldn't even finish my snap, never mind eat anything now.

[ALF *is standing with* KATH. KATH *is drinking her tea*]

KATH: I don't want anything happening to our Tony as well, you know, Alf.

ALF: I know that. But how could we stop him? What do you expect him to do when his dad's missing? It's only natural.

KATH: I know that. When anything like this happens it makes you nervous though, that's all. You start thinking all sorts.

[BEATSON *enters*]

BEATSON: Alf, can I have a word with you please, outside?

ALF: See you in a minute Kath.

[KATH *sits down again. The woman next to her has overheard her conversation with* ALF. *It is* MRS DOBSON, ALAN's *mother.* ALAN *is the lad in* SID's *team. Her husband is sitting at the other side of her*]

MRS DOBSON: Our Alan and your Tony were always in the same class together right from the infants, right through to leaving. Funny isn't it.... We should never have let him come to the pit. I was against it all along.

MR DOBSON: That's it, blame me.

MRS DOBSON: There's no point in blaming anybody now.

MR DOBSON: We both decided that if he did an engineering apprenticeship he'd be well qualified if he wanted to come out later.

MRS DOBSON: I know, but he didn't do an engineering apprenticeship, did he?

MR DOBSON: That's not my fault, is it? Anyway, he didn't have much choice with his qualifications, did he? Two CSEs, in Rural Studies and Art.

MRS DOBSON: I don't know. It makes you wonder what it's all for sometimes. You can talk to them until you're blue in the face and they'll still please themselves in the end.

[ALF *comes back into the room and walks across to* GEORGE KAY's WIFE, *says something to her, and they both leave the room. Everyone else in the room goes quiet*]

20: The pit yard

The BANKSMAN *opens the gate of the cage and two members of the Wakefield rescue team carry a stretcher out. There is a man strapped to it. His face is covered. They carry him across the pit yard towards the baths. TV cameramen and press photographers move forward and photograph them.* MRS KAY *is being helped out of the baths by* ALF *and* BEATSON. *She has her head down. She is crying quietly. The cameramen and photographers come forward and take her picture.*

21: The under manager's office

HARRY, *who has a bandaged head, and* STAN WALKER *are talking about* GEORGE KAY's *death.* ALF MEAKIN *and* CARTER *are also in the room.*

HARRY: You couldn't see a bloody thing, there was that much dust. You could feel it going into your mouth and up your nose, choking you. It was murder trying to breathe. Anyway, after I'd picked myself up and tried to phone the pit room, I set off up the gate and I heard somebody shouting. It was Stan and George. We decided what to do, then set off up the gate again. We couldn't see each other, the dust was that thick. It blocked your lamp out. We'd to travel by touch and shouting to each other. Stan was in front, I was next and George was at the back. When we got to the junction of Seven's main gate, we could smell burning, so we decided to go up the main gate and through the face. We set off, but when we reached the face there was only two of us, me and Stan. We'd lost George on the way. I don't know what happened to him. We never heard him shout or anything and the trouble was, we couldn't see each other. I don't know whether he collapsed or not.

ALF: Did you use your self-rescuers at all?

STAN: We put 'em on, and I used mine for a bit, but they're bloody murder, them things.

CARTER: The rescue team say that when they found George, he'd got his self-rescuer round his neck, but he hadn't got his mouthpiece in. He must have been wearing it and been overcome by the fumes and dust. When they tested the apparatus, they said there was still thirty-five minutes life left in it.

22: Underground

The colliery rescue team are digging at the fall in Seventeen's tail-gate. They are using picks and shovels and their bare hands to shift away the rocks and rubble. TONY is one of the men at work. After a few moments, WILF, the deputy looks at his watch.

WILF: Right lads, change over.

> [*The men who are working move back to make way for a fresh team. They are ready for a rest. TONY keeps on working flat out*]

WILF: Come on, Tony, give it a rest now.

TONY: I'm all right, Wilf. I'm just getting warmed up.

WILF: Listen, you'll be knackered if you carry on at this pace. It'll catch up with you in the end. You've got to look after yourself. What's the point in knocking yourself up in the first couple of hours when we might be at it all night?

TONY: Do you think we will be?

WILF: There's no telling. We'll just have to keep going until we break through.

> [*TONY moves away from the fall and goes to rest with the others. He takes a bottle of water from his jacket pocket, sits down, then has a long drink*]

TONY: What I don't understand is how it's affected this heading when the explosion's supposed to have happened on Fourteen's.

JIMMY: The blast gathers intensity, Tony. Quite often you get what they call a quiet zone, where the explosion's occurred. Surprisingly enough there's not a lot of damage there, but it gathers force and your worst damage can be hundreds of yards away. In such an enclosed space there's no way for it to disperse, you see. And if the explosion's strong enough to ignite any coal dust, you can get a flame travelling hundreds and hundreds of yards. Sometimes it can set the pit on fire if it's strong enough.

ERIC: At least that's one good thing: it seems to have snuffed itself out. There's no smell of burning anywhere.

WILF: A mate of mine worked at Gressley when the pit got on fire there. They'd to sandbag the whole district off to stop it spreading. It burned for a week. . . . Once anybody gets caught in anything like that they've no chance. Even if they don't get burned, they choke to death in no time.

TONY: Do you think there'll be any air getting through in there?

WILF: You can't say. We'll just have to hope for the best and work like bloody hell until we break through.

23: The canteen

Two miners, JOE *and* ROY, *are sitting at a table with* ALF MEAKIN *and the union official,* ACKROYD.

ACKROYD: Has there been any sign of gas down there lately?

ROY: There was a gas build-up on Twenty-ones and we had to withdraw men on there the other week.

JOE: And there was that incident on Ten's, when that cable got damaged in the main gate and started arcing. It was lucky nobody got injured then.

ACKROYD: Oh, aye, we heard about that one.

JOE: Things like that happen regular, things that nobody hears about, ordinary. Nobody gives a bugger as long as. . . .

ROY: Yea, but as far as I'm concerned, there wasn't anybody working on Fourteen's. The face was stood, wasn't it?

ALF: The deputy sent two fitters down to mend the motor.

ACKROYD: I bet they didn't test for gas, though, just the same.

ALF: Now, don't start jumping to conclusions. We don't know enough about it yet, do we?

ACKROYD: No, but we know enough about previous incidents. Men scuffling about, disregarding the safety regulations just for the sake of production. And management sitting there turning a blind eye and hoping for the best.

ALF: Now, let's not get carried away. We've no proof of negligence at this stage.

ROY: He's right. And I'll tell you something else as well. There wouldn't be half as many accidents if things were organized right instead of having to rely on incentives.

ALF: How do you mean?

ROY: Well, if we were in charge of the day-to-day running of things and we were responsible for setting the targets, safety would be bound to improve, wouldn't it? We'd make sure that safety and production went hand in glove. We'd feel it was more in our own interests then, wouldn't we?

ACKROYD: Well that's going to be the next big issue, isn't it – industrial democracy.

JOE: Well, that's got to come ... especially the strength that we've got now.

ACKROYD: Course it has.

ROY: We want to force it.

ACKROYD: Who were the fitters down there, anyway?

ALF: Well, one was Frank Morris and the other was an apprentice.

JOE: It's Steve Oates ... Charlie Oates's lad.

ROY: I know Frank well. He wouldn't do anything daft.

ACKROYD: Were they working together?

ALF: I suppose so. Why?

ACKROYD: Well, you know what happens. They get started on a job and something happens somewhere else. The deputy comes along, right, he pulls the man away and leaves the apprentice to finish off on his own. Now, I know it shouldn't happen, but it does.

JOE: Well, Frank Morris is a conscientious fella.

ROY: I don't think for one moment he'd leave young Oates on his own to do a job.

JOE: I know, but Ken Taylor was working under pressure, wasn't he?

ROY: Not half. The manager played hell with him over the tannoy. I heard that myself, this morning.

[CARTER *and* BEATSON *enter and join* ACKROYD *and* ALF MEAKIN *as the two miners get up to leave*]

JOE: There's no doubt about it – Ken Taylor was getting some stick to get that face working again.

ACKROYD: I'm glad you've come over. Look, we're going to need to know a bit more about this faulty motor that these fitters were looking at, you know.

CARTER: Well, it needed repairing.

ACKROYD: I know it needed repairing, but give me some details. What was wrong with it?

BEATSON: Well, it was damaged. I mean that's all I know about it. It was damaged and we sent somebody down to fix it. Geoff's got the report.

CARTER: It's all written down here, look. What happened was a cowl got damaged in a fall and we had to have a new one fitted.

ACKROYD: Cowl?

CARTER: Yes. Forbes played merry hell about it. He says there's always something going wrong with that face.

ALF: Well fitting a cowl's a straightforward enough job, isn't it?

ACKROYD: It is if it's done right.

CARTER: What do you mean by that?

ACKROYD: Exactly what I say. I just hope everything's going to be in order when we come to this inquiry, that's all.

BEATSON: Hey, now hold on, Brian, hold on. Let's not have these insinuations if you don't mind. All right? We do our job from up here you know.

ACKROYD: Oh, do you?

BEATSON: Yes we do, and we do it well. Look, you know as well as I do that it's impossible to make a pit 100 per cent fail-safe. Isn't it?

ACKROYD: What are you talking about?

BEATSON: Look, there's always that element that creeps in, there's bound to be an accident.

ACKROYD: Accident! I'm not talking about accidents, man. You know what Arthur Machin said at one inquiry, don't you? He said that most of the improvements to the safety regulations over the past one hundred years came about because of bloody disasters.

CARTER: What are you trying to say, Brian?

ALF: Look, if we're not careful someone's going to be saying a little bit too much here.

BEATSON: Yes, Alf's right.

[SHEILA, *the secretary, comes in*]

SHEILA: Excuse me, Mr Carter, Mr Johnson's just arrived.

CARTER: Oh, thanks, Sheila. Would you show him in, love?

[MR JOHNSON, *the MP, comes into the canteen*]

CARTER: Hello, Mr Johnson.

JOHNSON: Oh, hello.

CARTER: Pleased you could make it so quickly. You remember Phil Beatson.

[MR JOHNSON *greets everyone in the canteen*]

JOHNSON: I was told in the House, so I got the first plane up. Oh, this is a terrible business. What are the latest developments? I haven't heard anything since I left.

CARTER: Well, so far there's been one man brought out dead, so that leaves seven unaccounted for.

JOHNSON: Oh, well, let's hope they can be recovered safely. Well, is it possible to see Mr Forbes or....

CARTER: Shall I show you across? It's just across the yard, Mr Johnson.

[CARTER *and* JOHNSON *exit*]

ACKROYD: It's a wonder he knew his way here.

ALF: No, he was here last month for the visit.

ACKROYD: Was he? Well that's two disasters in a row then.

24: Underground

The Wakefield rescue team are searching Fourteen's district. They are not wearing their breathing apparatus. They come across an air door that has been blown down by the explosion.

RESCUER: Christ! It must have been some blast to blow that off like that.

[*They carry on. The* CAPTAIN *shines his lamp on the wall*]

CAPTAIN: It looks as though the flames travelled this far. There's signs of coking here, look.

[*They shine their lamps on the wall and discover coal dust that has been burned by the flames of the explosion. As they turn away to carry on they hear a voice*]

STEVE: Help! Help!

RESCUER 1: Hear that? There's somebody there.

[*They discover a man lying on his back at the side of the roadway. It is* STEVE OATES, *the apprentice electrician. Two members of the rescue team crouch down to attend to him*]

STEVE: What time is it?

CAPTAIN: Twenty to ten.

STEVE: What, in the morning.

CAPTAIN: At night. . . .

STEVE: Is that all? I thought I'd been lying here for days. . . .

CAPTAIN: Right, let's have that stretcher.

[*They ease* STEVE *on to the stretcher. He groans. He is badly injured. He has a broken leg and severe burns*]

RESCUER 2: You'll be all right now. We'll have you at the hospital in half an hour.

[*They strap him to the stretcher*]

CAPTAIN: Was there anybody else in this district with you?

STEVE: There was Ken Taylor and Frank Morris. We were looking for some pull lifts. The last time I saw 'em they were mending that motor on the conveyor.

CAPTAIN: Anybody else?

STEVE: Not that I know of.

CAPTAIN: Right lads, get him out. When you get to a tele-phone, phone the control room and tell them you're on the way out with an injured man and tell them to send a back-up team into Fourteen's after us.

[*Two of the rescue team pick up the stretcher*]

RESCUER: Are you comfortable enough?

STEVE: I'm champion ... I could do with a pint though.

[*The stretcher bearers carry off the injured man*]

25: Sid's house

MARK *is sitting with his legs up on the settee watching the television.* JANET *is trying to read a book. The programme ends.*

JANET: Come on now, Mark, it's time you were in bed. You'll be tired out in the morning.

MARK: I'm not going to bed until my mam comes home.

JANET: She said I'd to get you to bed in decent time if she wasn't back.

MARK: Well, I'm not going.

JANET: She'll be mad.

MARK: I'm not bothered. You can't make me go.

JANET: Go on, I'll wake you up as soon as she comes in.

MARK: No.

JANET: Well, lay down for a bit then.

[MARK *places a cushion against one of the arms of the settee and rests his head against it, still watching the television*]

MARK: They're a long time, aren't they, Janet? Do you think they'll be coming soon?

JANET: I shouldn't think they'll be long now.

[JANET *goes back to her book*]

MARK: Do you think anything's happened to my dad, Janet?

JANET: How do I know? We shall just have to hope for the best, won't we? . . .

MARK: It's rubbish, this programme. Turn it over to the other side, Janet.

JANET: Turn it off, more like. I'm supposed to be doing some homework. I've to read this chapter for tomorrow morning.

[*She switches to another channel on the television*]

26: Underground

The Wakefield rescue team – CAPTAIN, TWO RESCUERS *and* MAURICE *a younger lad – are near Fourteen's coal face. The* CAPTAIN *comes across a sheet of paper and picks it up.*

CAPTAIN: What's this?

[*They shine their lamps on it*]

It's a page out of a book. . . . They look like racehorse names to me.

[*He throws it down and they carry on to find another page a few yards further on*]

There's another one here, look. . . . There's something spilt on this one. . . . It's blood, I think.

RESCUER 1: It is blood.

[*He drops the page. The* CAPTAIN *shines his lamp on*

something on the floor. It looks like a piece of material.
He bends down and examines it, recoiling a little
when he discovers what it is]

CAPTAIN: Bloody hell.

RESCUER 1: What is it?

CAPTAIN: It's somebody's arm.

RESCUER 1: Jesus Christ.

[*Another member of the rescue team walks a few yards*
further on, shining his lamp on the ground. It finds
what looks like a pile of rags. It is a shattered body.
There are pages of the book scattered all around it]

RESCUER 2: There's somebody here.

[*The others come up to him and the* CAPTAIN *bends*
down to examine it. MAURICE, *one of the rescue party,*
turns away and moves back from the sight. He is too
distressed to look. There is the danger of him being
sick. While the CAPTAIN *is searching the shattered body*
for identification, the two other members of the team
move on]

RESCUER 1: There's another one here. [*Pause*] He's dead as
well.

CAPTAIN: There's no way of identifying him. He's blown to
bloody pieces. There's only his clothes holding him
together. I can't find his check or anything.

[*He realizes* MAURICE *is not feeling too good*]

CAPTAIN: Are you all right, Maurice?

MAURICE: Not bad.

CAPTAIN: I know how you feel, lad. We've all gone through
that at one time or another.

[*The other two* RESCUE WORKERS *come back and join*
them]

RESCUER 2: We've been right up to the end. There's only that one.

CAPTAIN: Right, lads, let's get them on the stretchers and get them out.

[*They prepare the stretchers, and the* CAPTAIN *and* MAURICE *bend down and place the shattered body of* FRANK MORRIS *on the stretcher while the other two walk away to fetch the other body. The* CAPTAIN *and* MAURICE *strap the body to the stretcher then make their way back*]

27: Beatson's office

The only people left are KATH, MRS KING *(*RONNIE's *wife) and* MR *and* MRS DOBSON *(*ALAN's *parents). They are subdued. They have been here a long time now. They are sick of drinking tea, eating the odd sandwich. Empty plastic cups and paper plates litter the desk and the window sills. The air is stale with cigarette smoke.*

MRS DOBSON: He's booked to go to Spain as well next week for a fortnight with his mates. He was right looking forward to it. He's never been abroad before. He was always scared of flying. But with a gang of 'em going it gave him a bit of courage. They've never flown either.... Oh, Shaun Davies has, I think. He went to play football on the Isle of Man at Easter, and they flew there.

MR DOBSON: I bet he wishes they'd have gone this week. He'd have been sat in a bar now, brown as a berry, getting a few pints down him.

MRS DOBSON: Red as a beetroot, more like. You know how the sun affects his skin....

MRS KING: You can't believe it really, can you? It doesn't seem real.

MRS DOBSON: I'll tell you one thing. If he does come out of this all right, he's not going back down the pit, that is a certainty. I'd sooner him be on the dole than let him go back down there.

MRS KING: Our Ronnie only came off the dole last month. He was on the dole for six months after they closed Melton Main down. There was nothing else going though. He'd no choice really.

MRS DOBSON: They talk about one hundred pound a week. I wouldn't let him go back down for a thousand a week after this. It's just not worth it, I don't care what you say.

[*Pause*]

MRS KING: It gets you down, don't it, all this waiting?

MRS DOBSON: I'll tell you what, though: I'd sooner be here than stuck in bed badly like Albert's wife. It'd drive me crackers, would that.

MRS KING: I suppose so.... But then you dread 'em coming to fetch you just in case something's happened.... You can't win, can you?

MR DOBSON: You know what they say, don't you? No news is good news.

MRS DOBSON: Don't you start, Ken, with what folks say. It's enough to get on anybody's nerves.

[*A* SALVATION ARMY WOMAN *enters*]

SA WOMAN: Anyone like a cup of tea? We've got plenty in the van.

MRS KING: No thanks, love.

MRS DOBSON: If I have any more tea it'll be running out of my ears.

[*The* SA WOMAN *looks at* KATH *and goes over to her*]

SA WOMAN: It's Kath Walshaw, isn't it?

[KATH *looks round at her, surprised*]

KATH: That's right.... I don't think I know you, though, do I?

[KATH *tries to place the face after all this time*]

KATH: Maureen. I didn't know you.

MAUREEN: It's been a long time, Kath.

KATH: Fancy, after all these years.

[*They smile at each other. They are both suddenly shy*]

KATH: So you stopped in the Army, then?

MAUREEN: That's right.

KATH: Just think. And we only went to their youth club that night because Roger Marshall was going to be there.

[*They both laugh at the memory*]

KATH: I wonder what happened to him?

MAUREEN: He went away to University, didn't he?

KATH: That's right, I think he did.

MAUREEN: And you married Sid.

KATH: How do you know?

MAUREEN: I keep in touch. My mother still lives on East Bank, you know. I come over sometimes.

KATH: I've never seen your mother for ages now.

MAUREEN: He was a nice lad, Sid. He once gave Roy Marples a black eye for calling me specky four eyes.... I know he's still down there, Kath. Let's hope to God that everything turns out all right.

[KATH *turns away, choked*]

KATH: Thanks, love. I'll see you later.

[MAUREEN *goes out as a* REPORTER *enters*]

REPORTER: Excuse me, I wonder if I could have a few words with you?

KATH: What about?

REPORTER: Your husband's still trapped underground, isn't he?

KATH: Are you a reporter?

REPORTER: Yes, I'm with ...

KATH: I don't care who you're with. I've nothing to say to you.

REPORTER: I can understand your feelings. Perhaps when it's all over, say tomorrow sometime, I could call round at your house and we could have a chat then?

[KATH *does not answer him. She just looks at him. The* REPORTER *is forced to go on*]

REPORTER: We'll pay you, of course. The story will be exclusive to us.

KATH: You've a cheek. Honestly. I don't know how you've the nerve.

REPORTER: What do you mean?

KATH: Come round our house! You'd better not, or you're likely to find yourself with a thick ear.

REPORTER: There's no need to be like that about it. I only....

KATH: You make me poorly, you lot. You come up here, writing sob stories, reckoning to sympathize, but you don't care a damn really. Just wait 'til it all dies down and we put in for another pay rise, it'll be a different tale then, won't it? It'll be greedy miners, or a communist conspiracy. We'll be holding the country to ransom again. Anything to turn people against us. You weren't writing sob stories about us in the '72 and '74 strikes, were you? You didn't want to come round to our house then.... You just tell lies, that's all, and I don't want anything to do with you.

[*She hurriedly leaves the office*]

28: Sid's house

MARK *is asleep on the settee and* JANET *is reading in the chair. She looks across at* MARK, *puts her book on the chair arm, gets up and turns the television off then walks across to him.*

JANET: Mark. [*Pause*] Mark.

> [*He stirs and mumbles.* JANET *bends down and picks him up. He is heavy but she manages*]

JANET: Come on. Let's have you up to bed.

> [*She takes him out of the room*]

29: Beatson's office

KATH *enters the room, now more composed than when she was speaking to the* REPORTER. *The three people inside tense and look towards the door.*

MR DOBSON: Any news?
KATH: Nothing new.

> [*She sits down.* MR DOBSON *lights a cigarette.* MRS DOBSON *closes her eyes.* MRS KING *rests her head on her hands and looks at the floor.* KATH *looks straight ahead, awake, alert, waiting*]

30: Underground

The Doncaster rescue team are sitting in a line against the wall resting. Two have their eyes closed. Nobody is talking. The men can hear work being carried out at the face in the distance. There is a pause, the sound of work stops, then the two men who have been working at the face are heard coming down the gate. One of the resting men sits up and looks towards their approaching lights.

RESCUER 3: Bloody hell, it's not time to change already is it? They've only been at it ten minutes.

[*The two men reach the Doncaster team and take off their breathing apparatus quickly. They are out of breath*]

RESCUER 4: We're through! It's clear!

[*Everybody in the rescue team jumps up and gathers round the two rescuers eager for information*]

31: The general manager's office

FORBES *is sitting at his desk.* CARTER *stands looking out of the window. The phone rings. He picks it up immediately.*

FORBES: ... All four? ... What about their checks? ... Wait a minute.

[*He finds a pen on his desk and places a sheet of paper in front of him. While he is listening, he is writing something down on the paper*]

... Right ... Right, Tom, we'll check that straight-away.

[*He puts the phone down*]

FORBES: They've found them. Two of them are dead, two still alive. They're in a bad way by the sounds of it and both unconscious but they're alive. They're receiving emergency treatment before they move them any further. They're on their way out with the other two. They've identified two of them: Albert Rhodes, he's dead, and the lad Alan Dobson, he's still alive, thank God. It's the other two, they've lost their checks. The dead man is in a pretty bad state apparently. We need to find out who he is before we ask the relatives to identify him. We don't want to make things any worse by giving somebody's wife the wrong news.

[*He goes out of the office taking the sheet of paper with him*]

32: Beatson's office

BEATSON *hesitantly enters*.

BEATSON: Mrs King, could I have a word for a moment?

[*The others, seeing the look on* BEATSON's *face leave the room*]

MRS KING: Is there any news, Mr Beatson?

BEATSON: Well, we've found them, but we're not sure of their identities yet. We're just finding out who's who.

MRS KING: Is he all right?

BEATSON: Was your Ronnie wearing a pair of green football socks at all?

MRS KING: Green football socks? What's he want to be wearing football socks for? He's never played a game of football in his life as far as I know.

BEATSON: What about a signet ring? Was he wearing a gold signet ring?

MRS KING: He does wear a ring. Why?

BEATSON: A square one, with a criss-cross pattern on one side?

MRS KING: That's right. He got it for his twenty-first birthday. . . .

BEATSON: I'm afraid I've got some bad news for you, Mrs King. I think you'd better sit down.

[*There is a moment as she realizes what the bad news is. Then she buckles at the knees and starts to cry.* BEATSON *gets hold of her and sits her down*]

33: The pit bank

The cage comes slowly to the surface. The BANKSMAN *opens the gate and lets the men out. It is the volunteer rescue team which had tried to clear the fall in the heading.* TONY *and* JIMMY *are amongst them. Nobody is talking. The men are exhausted. The* REPORTERS *speak to* ACKROYD, *the NUM official.* KATH *enters and* ALF MEAKIN *goes over to speak to her.*

ALF: You want to get off home now, Kath. I'll get you a lift if you want.

KATH: I'll wait for our Tony, Alf. We might as well go home together.

ALF: I suppose so. Jesus Christ, I hope I've never to go through anything like this again. I've heard about folks going grey overnight, and I can understand why now.

34: Beatson's office

BEATSON: Well, I suppose I'd better get off and tell Albert's wife. I suppose there'll be somebody up now.

FORBES: She's not in the house on her own, is she?

BEATSON: No, she's a daughter looking after her.... I'll get off home then and get a bit of sleep.

FORBES: Yes. I've got these telegrams. I'll just stay and have a look at them.

[BEATSON *leaves the room.* FORBES *just sits there. He is so exhausted, he is in a daze. The room is littered with empty cardboard cups. He slowly opens the telegrams*]

35: Sid's house

JANET *is asleep on the settee. There is the sound of the kitchen door being opened. She opens her eyes just as* KATH *and* TONY *come into the room.*

JANET: What's happened, mam? Where's my dad?

KATH: They've taken him to hospital.

JANET: Is he all right?

KATH: He's alive. That's the main thing.
[JANET *puts her head in her hands*]

KATH: He's got a broken leg, broken pelvis and he's badly burned on his chest and arms. He was still unconscious when they brought him out. I'm going to ring through to the hospital in a bit, see how he's going on. I'll go down there later on when I've got you and our Mark off to school.

TONY: [*To* JANET] What you crying for? He'll be all right now. Better than five I could name anyroad.
[MARK *has been awakened by their voices. He comes into the room in his pyjamas*]

MARK: What's our Janet crying for? Where's my dad?

KATH: He's all right, love. He's been injured in an accident at the pit. They've taken him to the hospital.
[*She goes over to him and holds him to her*]

MARK: How long will he be in? Will he be better in time to take me to the Test Match next week?
[TONY *grins*]

JANET: You selfish thing! Who's bothered about cricket matches when he's nearly been killed?

MARK: I didn't know, did I?

TONY: I'll take you, Mark. You, me and your Uncle Harry'll go. Then when my dad's better he can take you to a county match later on.

MARK: I know. But it'll not be same as going with my dad, will it?
[KATH *tries to stop herself crying by keeping her lips together. Tears come into her eyes, which she hides from the others by going over to the window and tidying the curtains. It is morning now, full light*]

THE LIBRARY
SAINT FRANCIS XAVIER
SIXTH FORM COLLEGE
MALWOOD ROAD, SW12 8EN